# ZEN AND THE ART OF DYING

By

Jared Wynn

**Special thanks, in no particular order, to:**

My wife, Yuying Chen-Wynn, for saying yes.

My parents, Jeff and Louise, for raising me the way they did.

My siblings, Lisa, Valerie, Cory, and DonRaphael, for putting up with my childhood antics.

The Skiddos, AKA my step kids, for putting up with my many adulthood antics.

Garrett Scott Von Gunten for the combat vocabulary consult.

The RevPit contest and editors: https://reviseresub.com/

And especially Sione Aeschliman, for being a better editor than I could have even hoped for: https://www.writelearndream.com/

"You have to die a few times before you can live."

- Charles Bukowski

# 1

Last night and six lifetimes ago, I picked what I thought would be a nice, quiet spot to bed down for a bit of beauty rest. It was by a dumpster in an alley; relatively rat-free and with just a soupçon of urine, enough to know the cops don't come around often but not so much as to put me off my breakfast. Speaking of which, did I mention the dumpster? It belongs to a Michelin-rated restaurant with a signature saffron marsala sauce, so that plate of pasta no one ever seems to finish, that was going to be my breakfast when I woke up.

But then I started craving a muffin instead. Maybe because I can no longer tell the difference between here and now and late afternoon last Tuesday, or perhaps it has something to do with the ambience of the alley. But whatever the case may be, the craving was real. I swear it wasn't just an excuse to get a glimpse of her.

BAM! The dumpster lid goes down like a gunshot and my eyes slam open. I look up to see the old familiar face of another loser like me. I've been waking up to his ugly mug for almost a week now, but he wouldn't know that.

"Sorry man," he says. "Just grabbing a bite to eat. You want something?" he asks as he lifts the lid again.

"I told you, I don't have time to stick around and chit-chat," I say.

He looks at me sideways like he always does.

"What you mean, you told me? You even know my name?"

"Your friends call you Meatball." I say while standing and scanning the street outside the alley. "Because you once made a bet you could get anything for anyone, so someone asked you to get them a meatball sandwich from a restaurant that didn't sell sandwiches."

The clock on the bank across the street reads 8:50, so I duck back behind the dumpster while finishing Meatball's life story for him. "They thought you were going to embarrass yourself, but you went in, made friends with the staff, got them to make you one from scratch, and now it's their best-selling item. But you don't remember telling me any of that, do you?"

I hear a car idling slowly by. Something about the occupant and the way he's peering into the alley spooks Meatball, and I can't say I blame him. It's why I'm hiding.

When Meatball turns to look at me with wide eyes, I know the coast is clear, so I get up.

"I tell you you could also stand to learn some people skills?" Meatball asks.

The clock on the bank says 8:51.

"Too late," I say as I take off running.

# 2

Her phone vibrates violently in her pocket, breaking the rhythm of her stride and startling her so hard it rings for a full five seconds before she can stop fishing around in her purse and remember where she put it. A million thoughts cross her mind in the half second that it takes to pull the phone out and look at the screen. Is she needed? Does she need to be needed? And why can't she remember where she put her phone even when she can feel it buzzing in her pocket, is she really that hopeless before her first cup of coffee?

All those thoughts are washed away in a flood of dread when she sees the number on the screen. She told him no. She told him no means no. And then she told him nothing, she didn't answer his texts or pick up, even letting her voicemail fill up to the point where he couldn't leave another grunting soliloquy about how much she meant to him and love and belonging and blah blah blah. She thought he would have gotten the hint by now.

That sense of dread is replaced with a sudden thread of hope and happiness when she sees an older gentleman converging on her path. It looks like he's trying to head her off so he can get ahead of her in the line. She sprints the last fifteen feet or so and beats him by inches with an insistent grin that says 'no, after you,' as she holds the door for him, and he rewards her with surprised and smiling eyes. Today's going to be a good day because karma's her bitch.

Her phone starts vibrating again; she wonders for a moment whether she should answer it, but life is too short to let something like this drag her down. So she opts instead to step inside and get on with the rest of her existence.

As she steps through the door, the phone in her hand suddenly goes as still and quiet as every customer in the shop.

Except one.

# 3

Step to the left, jump to the right, and roll.

The guy in the car, the one who spooked Meatball, his name is Santo, and he's part of the reason I'm doing this. But I don't want to think about that right now, I really need to focus on not getting shot. Having a bullet rip through me ranks right up there with getting raped and going to the DMV; it's not exactly something someone puts on their bucket list.

So, step to the left, jump to the right, and roll, I chant to myself while running across the street and up the adjacent alley.

I startle the owner of a struggling restaurant as he's taking out the trash, and he scurries back into his kitchen with a look of alarm. He caught me rooting through his dumpster once and threw food at me, which made about as much sense as spanking a fetishist. I keep wanting to tell him he'll do a lot better in business if he throws food at the paying customers instead, but he ducks behind the steel door and locks it, and I'm out of breath anyway.

Step to the left. Jump to the right. Roll.

Wish I had time to practice, but the first time I came this way, I only recognized her by the knock-off designer purse under her arm; most of her face and the space behind it was already spread out all over a wall. Fortunately, her killer had another round in the chamber, so I was able to come back and save her, but I still only got there in time to watch her get murdered. The third time, I ran so fast that I practically died, right before I actually died. And it still took me a few more tries before I figured out the pattern.

But the seventh time's the charm, right?

I emerge from the alley into a world of winners at the game of life, all hurrying to punch a clock and win just a little bit more. Some of them look at me with a face that screams "you don't belong here." Some of them are looking inwardly at themselves with that same face.

I wish someone among them could have looked at her and realized she was in trouble.

Oh, and this "her" of whom I speak, well. There she is. Cady DeClaire. Curvy, nerdy, and so beautiful she'd take my breath away if I wasn't already out of it. She's holding the door to the coffee shop for another customer, happily being herself without thinking or worrying about who or what might be waiting for her just inside. And why should she? She thinks today's a day like any other, and in a way it is. Every day, dozens of women die the way she's about to.

I mean, the way she *was* about to. Thing is, I owe her a little favor. So right after she walks into the coffee shop, I close my eyes and follow.

# 4

Closing my eyes helps me adjust faster to the darker interior, which in turn helps me dodge a terrified customer cowering on the floor. Which in turn helps me dodge a bullet.

A 230-grain lump of lead flies by my face, as I knew it would. I don't need to look to see the damage done to the door behind me; that same piece of metal went through my eye and out the back of my mind once.

"Freeze!" he yells, and I comply, hands up in a defensive posture. He doesn't know what I am yet and

I need to keep it that way for just a couple more moments while I get into position.

"Who the fuck are you!" he screams, or at least that's what I think he's screaming. It's hard to make out words, but I can make out rage through the ringing in my ears.

And I can make out Cady on the floor, holding her hand over her bruised cheek. He was waiting for her.

Oh, and by "he," I'm referring to Cady's ex-boyfriend. I don't know his name, where he's from, or why he's such an asshole, but I know everything that matters in this moment. I know he's holding a Kimber SIS .45 caliber semiautomatic pistol, I know there are at least two more rounds in that thing, and I know he's planning on getting those rounds out of that hard steel chamber and into some soft warm people. And, most importantly, I know he's spent a lot of time practicing for this moment.

Most civilians have no clue just how hard it is to hit a target, but some people train to the point where they could put a bullet through an actual bull's eye without batting a lash and this guy just happens to be one such person. Which means if I screw up this next move, a piece of compressed lead designed to punch back as much as through a person will do both to me so fast I won't know which is which. And have I mentioned just how much I hate dying?

I take a step forward, clearing the entryway. "Don't even think about it!" he screams.

"I'm not thinking about anything," I reply while taking another tentative step. If this is going to work, I need him to think I'm just looking for a safe spot on the floor with the other cowering customers. And they're understandably terrified; as far as they know, they could die right now and it'll all be over. Their hopes, their dreams, their regrets... they're lucky.

His finger goes white on the trigger. I'm almost there.

"You know her? You do, don't you?" he asks, pointing at Cady with the gun.

"Yeah, she's my ex-college roommate's uncle's dog sitter's niece's second cousin twice removed. You?"

I'm still slowly inching forward, trying my best to look like I'm shaking in fear. It helps that I am.

"She didn't tell me about you!" His voice goes up in pitch and is even a bit raspier now. Sheesh, how much adrenaline can that big body produce? Step to the left, jump to...

"Please, don't... he'll kill you..." Cady whimpers from the floor. She recognizes me, and she's probably regretting having ever met me, but I can't dwell on that. The slightest distraction right now could get us both killed. At least that's been my experience.

I take one more step and meet his eyes finally. And smile. "There's a lot she didn't tell you." It's OK, I'm in position now so I can piss him off. I think.

He points the gun at her for a moment, hesitates, then decides to murder me first. So far so good.

I take a big step forward and to the left and BAM! Everything feels like I'm wading through water in slow motion but I still can't see the bullet that slams through the space where my heart was.

He swings the gun to his right as I take a big jump forward and to my right and BAM! He overcompensates and misses me again.

BAM! He undercompensates this time while zeroing in. This'll be my last shot at not getting shot, so I duck and roll the last few feet...

... and bowl myself right into his knees as two more rounds go into the floor behind me. He falls backward, hitting his head on the counter as I continue to roll up onto and all over him, wrenching his arm back in the process.

He drops the gun and tries to shrimp away, looking for just a second like one of the terrified customers cowering into a corner.

I pick up the gun and smash it into his head over and over again until he stops moving. Yeah, I know, I could kill him right now and everyone would call me a hero. But I want to put an idea between his ears more than a bullet, and that idea is really simple: don't hurt people.

I hit him one more time to make my point.

Then, suddenly for the first time in a very short week, I don't know what's going to happen next. Maybe I'll watch the sun set tonight. Maybe I'll find a new dumpster, perhaps something behind an Indian restaurant. Speaking of breakfast, I could really go for the usual right now, and this place has the best blueberry crumb muffins you can imagine. I mean, if you could die and come back for any one thing, it'd be one of those muffins. But don't take it from me just because I've done precisely that.

I stand up and check myself for holes.

"Hey," she says, looking at me with bewilderment. She starts to get up as my entire world comes crashing back down. The look in her eyes echoes the feeling in my heart. Who the hell am I and what the hell am I doing here?

Gotta try and look dignified while I make my exit, so I hand her the gun butt-first, pick up a muffin, and then do my best to ignore all the eyes on me as I walk toward the door.

"Hey!" she says a little louder. I turn to see she's pointing at me with the gun, so I force a smile and point back with my thumb cocked like we're at the OK Corral.

She suddenly notices the instrument of death in her hand and recoils, setting it down with a clunk on the counter while asking "that's it?"

"Yeah. Just the muffin this time. Thank you."

I turn back to the freshly ventilated door and put one foot in front of the other like any other customer who's late for work. I'll get my shit together later, but right now, I just need to get from point A to point B. And right now, point B is out of here.

# 5

I step out into the morning sun as a surreal emotional soup of awe and wonder and relief and regret washes over me. I need to move before the cops come, but I'm still too emotional to start. The air is crisp, the shadows are long, and everything smells like heaven. Oh wait, that's the muffin in my hand.

I should be used to cheating death by now, but cheating it the old fashioned way is still so much better than waking up to Meatball's ugly mug. Tomorrow will be a whole new day and a whole new dumpster, but today, I just need to find a place far from here to enjoy this feeling. And this muffin. I take a bite and savor the buttery blueberry goodness.

And then I turn to run, only to run right into Santo.

I drop my breakfast.

"Why do I feel like you're avoiding me?" he asks.

I spit a mouthful of breakfast into his face and take off in the other direction. Or try to; he has a handful of my shirt in one hand while he's trying to wipe premasticated muffin out of his eyes with the other. I'll give him this, he's fast.

But he's also blind, and I owe him a hundred lifetimes of hate, so I hit him in the face as hard as I can.

He lets me go, and go is what I'm good at. I don't need to look to know he's running too, I can hear his feet rhythmically pounding the pavement like boxing gloves on a heavy bag behind me. He's bigger and his legs are longer, but his heart's still standard issue, and right now that heart is struggling to pump blood through a lot more vascular yardage. He'll run out of gas before I do.

But as I sprint past a florist's shop, I knock a display of potted plants in terra cotta vases into his path anyway. I don't think this'll slow him down, it's just one of those movie moments I've been wanting to check off my bucket list. Now if I can just get into a car chase and drive through a fruit stand, I can die happy for once.

I run across a street and up an alley into another world, away from all the angry commuters and brainwashed office drones and back into the realm of the pandemic homeless and chronic addicts and other forgotten people. It takes me a moment, but I realize I'm no longer hearing his feet behind me. Then it takes me another moment to process that realization.

I slow down enough to risk a peek behind and find that I'm alone sooner than I thought I would be. Did he give up already? Or trip over a petunia back at the flower shop? I'm not complaining; in all the heat of the chase I forgot where I was and ran up the wrong alley. This one's a dead end.

Which is fine, because you know what, I'm done here. This alley, this neighborhood, this town. Time to find a new life in a new city, with new alleys and different dumpsters. Or who knows? Maybe I'll find a new job, and a coffee shop to go with it. Some place with really good lemon scones, for man doth not live on blueberry muffins alone. I'm going to start over, get off the streets, spend more time living and less time dying.

First step is getting out of this alley unseen. No doubt he's still out there.

A car screeches to a stop at the entrance of the alley. I recognize that car.

I race up the alley, gotta try to clear that thing before he can get out and get me.

But it's too far. He's already out, coming around, coming into the alley. Time for plan B. Time to come up with a plan B. Or think of a word that starts with the letter B.

"Back off!" I shout.

He keeps coming at me with his hands out in front of him. It looks like he's either begging me to listen or getting ready to grab me. I know better than to give him the benefit of the doubt.

"I'm not going back!" I say.

"I'm not asking you to!" he answers.

"Please!" My voice goes up high with my hands in hot pursuit. "Please... You have no idea what it was like in there!"

"Will you just shut up and listen to me for five minutes?" He keeps walking toward me while I keep walking backward. The only thing I know to do when cornered is lure the attacker in and lash out. But he's coming in, lured or not, and unlike Cady's boyfriend, Santo knows what I am. So he's not going to fall for the old terrified-of-dying routine. I'm just going to have to lash out without it.

I bump off the wall behind me and slam into Santo, battering him with my hands and feet and more hate than he can handle. This is easier than I thought, he isn't even hitting back. He goes down and I go over him.

And then I go down, face-first, into the pavement. I feel and hear a familiar squishy-crunchy sensation in my face, followed by a searing pain that shoots up into my sinuses and wraps around my eyeballs. My nose is the first thing to get smashed whenever I tangle with one of these assholes.

Then I feel like I'm being pulled back, and it isn't just a feeling. I was too busy face-butting asphalt to notice this a moment ago, but Santo's got me by the ankle.

I turn over and around just in time to get him between my legs in what grapplers call the guard. If it looks like he's on top, that's only because you think you're right-side up. Even though gravity tells me I'm the bitch, I've got him straddled so I've got the leverage. Unless he's bigger, which he is, and unless he's stronger, which...

He picks me up and slams me back down while getting an arm between his body and my leg. Being pounded into the pavement doesn't feel as bad as it sounds; that elbow in my femoral nerve cavity actually hurts a lot more. But at least he's working on my legs now. So his hands are down.

I bring both my palms together on either side of his head like a pair of crashing cymbals. If I'm lucky, I'll find out I ruptured his ear drum. If I'm even luckier, I'll get away and spend the rest of forever not knowing.

I get up and run. He gets my ankle again. At least this time I'm able to land in a push-up position; I donkey-kick backward, trying my best to knock the wind out of him while pushing off and giving myself a head start, but he anticipates this, pulling backward with his entire body and adding momentum to my kick. He pivots to move out of the way while pulling, but he doesn't move enough. My chin slams into his knee, clapping my molars together and sending a sick shock up into my brain. I catch a glimpse of glitter on the asphalt, stars moving in and out of focus as my face flies through them.

We collapse together into an awkward pile on the pavement, rolling around in our sweat and years of caked-on oil and carbon exhaust that leaches out whenever it rains. Except I'm not really rolling as much as I'm being rolled. Reminds me of that old proverb about the difference between sleeping and being asleep, screwing and being screwed... I can't remember how it goes. I can't even remember where I am or what I'm doing. I'm aware of the grease and grime around me and Santo's engine idling in the background and nothing else.

# 6

I'm sitting in the passenger seat of a black two-door coupe with an all-leather interior, custom sound system, and an asshole at the wheel. The asshole looks at me nervously like he's afraid I might start spewing my breakfast or the meaning of life all over the inside of his vehicle. I'm trying to parse through a dreamlike impression in the back of my mind of him bundling me in and fastening the seatbelt. I lift the seatbelt strap off my chest to look at it and realize it's slick with my drool. He looks relieved when he notices this.

"Syrup?" he asks.

The traffic outside sounds like I'm hearing it through a pool of syrup, but that's just the blood in my throat and sinuses. I swallow a big coppery lump of it and say "no thanks, just the waffles."

"What? No, I said, so Europe."

I used to wonder whether people wore seatbelts in hell. Now I just nod, knowing they do.

"Good, so you're up."

I wasn't down, I was dazed. And now I'm confused; what's the proper social etiquette in a situation like this, should I talk about the weather? Is it too soon to start gouging his eyes out? Or if I were to just open the door and jump, would that hurt his feelings? We're not going too fast or too slow, so at this rate, I'm sure it'd hurt mine.

"Hand, Purell ease out Hobbit."

"What the hell?" I ask. Wish he'd stop pounding verbal nails into my brain so I could catch up with my train of thought.

"I said, man, you're really out of it."

I recognize this particular stretch of highway; it was probably a parking lot about an hour ago.

"Kenny," he says. That's my name, by the way. Kenny Mulligan. My mom used to tell me my name meant life was about second chances. Easy for her to say, she didn't have to grow up with a last name that means you suck at whacking balls.

"Kenny, you all right?"

"What's up with the traffic here?" My head's getting clearer now.

"All that and you're asking about the traffic? What is up with you? You used to be a fighter!"

"I wasn't a fighter, I was an escaper."

"Well, I'm an escaper too, now. I quit."

He waits a while for me to react. I let him.

"I don't work there anymore," he continues. "I've been trying to find you, tell you what's going on."

"How many are there?" Curiosity finally gets me. You could say I've been dying to ask this question and it wouldn't exactly be a figure of speech.

"We interviewed a lot of people."

"How many like me?"

"A lot. But you're the only one who got out while I was there. Which is why I need to talk to you."

"No, thanks."

"You don't want to try and fix this? Undo what they did to you?"

"They?"

"OK, I deserve that. I'm sorry, OK? I'm sorry."

Santo turns his eyes back to the road just in time to see the light turn red. He brakes hard, pushing me forward into the seatbelt. I undo the seatbelt and try the door at the same time, but the child lock is engaged. The window doesn't open either.

"Hey, just. Come with me, hear me out. I'll feed you, get you cleaned up. Or not, that's up to you, but at least just hear me out, OK?"

I stare at all the traffic signs and litter and freedom on the other side of this sixth inch of tempered glass.

"You're not immortal," he says. Funny, my mom used to say the same thing every time I undid my seatbelt.

"You know what's going to happen to you when you die," he says as the light turns green. He accelerates hard, right up to the speed limit before leveling off like a good little citizen.

"Kenny," he says. Once, when I was a kid, I wrote 'I've been kidnapped' on a piece of paper and held it up to the window of my mom's station wagon while she was driving. She didn't think it was so funny when she got pulled over, but what I wouldn't give for a marker and piece of paper right now.

"Kenny," he says a little louder.

"Why are you going so slow?" I ask.

"What? I'm going fifty-five."

I try to fix him with my best you're-such-a-wuss look, but with my broken nose I feel more like a tourist trying to order French food. But at least I'm controlling the conversation.

"Why do you think speed limits fall on the fives?"

"What the hell are you talking about?"

"Like why is it always fifty-five or sixty-five but not sixty?"

"I don't know. Some politician thought he could shave a few miles and save a few lives. Is there anyone in my blind spot?"

I look over my shoulder at the empty space in his blind spot and lie. "Yeah."

"Listen, I'm sorry about what happened. I swear to you, I had no idea they were going to treat you like that."

There's a tunnel coming up ahead and everyone in the oncoming lane is driving like people do when they come out of a tunnel: faster. I need to keep him in this lane.

"You keep saying they."

"And I'll keep saying I'm sorry until you believe me, but Kenny, this is bigger than both of us!"

He signals a lane change so I pretend to check his blind spot for him again. "Not yet," I caution. If I time this right, I won't have to wait for my nose to heal.

"They're recruiting," he says. "You know what that means?"

"Speed up, you can pass him," I say while looking over my shoulder at the imaginary car in his blind spot.

"Last thing I need right now is to get pulled over. They have a cop on the payroll, in case you didn't know."

Santo finally turns to check his blind spot and realizes no one's there. We lock eyes. All I can do now is hope that fifty-five is fast enough.

I grab the wheel and lean in with all my body, turning us directly into the path of a truck in the oncoming lane. Its headlights fill the car along with Santo's screams, washing over me until everything goes white.

And then everything goes black.

# 7

BAM! The dumpster lid goes down like a gunshot and my eyes slam open. This isn't the new day and dumpster I was hoping for, but it's better than being Santo's blowup doll. I look up and see an old familiar face.

"Sorry man," Meatball says. "Just grabbing a bite to eat. You want something?"

I jump up in alarm, take a deep breath and feel my nose, which isn't broken. Technically, it never was.

"You late for work or something?" He's looking at me like I'm about to declare myself the New and Improved Queen of England.

Every segment of society has its lowest ranking members just like every ladder has its lowest rung. In the military, a private fresh out of basic training is the one everybody steps on. In politics, it's anyone with morals. Among the homeless, it's the sort of people who say they died so they could travel back in time to save a girl.

I can't have him giving off the wrong vibe when Santo drives by, so I try to pretend I wasn't just feeling up my nose and put on my best aw-shucks smile.

"You know what they say, when you live to see another day."

"Are you living?" he asks.

"I don't even know anymore." The clock on the bank says 8:50, so I duck back behind the dumpster.

"Shit, that's a good thing. Means you're starting to see through the illusion! My name's Meatball."

"And what kind of name is Meatball?" I ask, even though I already know the answer.

"Swedish!" he cackles with laughter while diving back into the dumpster, emerging a moment later with a handful of actual meatballs. "I can't believe they throw these out! You want some?" They're the same color as the dirt and grime caked into his hands and under his nails. Just looking at those meat droppings makes me long for some expired produce. I politely shake my head while reminding myself for the umpteenth time that I need to start hanging out behind grocery stores.

"I didn't even use to like these," he says as he turns them over in his hand like a jeweler appraising big fleshy diamonds. "But I made a bet once, said I could get anyone anything they wanted 'cause I got people skills. So this friend of mine, she bet me I couldn't get her a meatball sandwich. I said come on, that's easy! But she said no, you gotta get it from a particular place."

"Let me guess," I interject. "A particular place that didn't even use to sell a meatball sandwich?" They say repetition is the key to learning, but I've heard this story about a damn sandwich a half a dozen times already and haven't learned a goddamned thing.

"They didn't sell any kind of sandwich!" He exclaims, almost dropping a meatball in the process. "At least they didn't use to. But I went inside, made some friends, taught them how to make one from ingredients they had, and then here's the thing..."

"They've been carrying it on their menu ever since," I finish for him.

He looks at me sideways like he always does. And suddenly, I realize I should have heard Santo's car idling past by now.

"That's a nice tattoo you got there," he says as I stand and peek out from my hiding spot. He's pointing to the blue and grey yin and yang on my arm, a symbol of an impulsive choice I once made which I've spent the rest of my life regretting. It's not something I talk about. Not even with homeless people named after sandwiches.

"What's your name?" he asks as I run to the entrance of the alley and look around.

The clock on the bank says 8:52.

"Shit," I say as I take off running.

"Now what the hell kind of name is that?" I can hear him laughing behind me as I race across the street and up the adjacent alley.

# 8

The owner of the struggling restaurant sees me barreling up the alley but he's already back in his kitchen, so he just watches me nonchalantly through the steel grate door. Funny what a difference a minute and twenty pounds of metal can make.

Santo's out there somewhere, and he isn't even the worst thing that's looking for me right now.

I thought that if I never spent another night in the same place twice and resigned myself instead to a life of misery and loneliness, they would never find me.

But then I remembered how much I liked those muffins, which led to remembering how much I liked a person who once bought me one.

So, step to the right, jump to the left... No, that's not right, first step is to the left. She'll die if I screw this up.

She's going to die anyway, someday, and that fact doesn't escape me. But the thing about dying, after you take away everything everyone thinks they know or don't know about it, there are only two opinions worth having: either you're looking forward to it or you aren't. And even though I've already been through all the sorts of things that can make a person hope for heaven or long for oblivion, I still fall into the latter category. And so, I assume, does Cady. Which is why I want to save her again.

Or die trying again, I think to myself as I crash through the door of the coffee shop and into the middle of Cady's boyfriend's you-made-me-do-this speech.

I trip over one of the terrified customers and go flying across the room, right into the asshole's asshole, causing him to lose his balance and hit his head on the counter. He drops the gun and proceeds to just lie there without even so much as the common courtesy of a swear word.

I can't pick up the gun, I can't hit him over the head, I can't think, I can't breathe. I can't believe I never tried this before. All that trying and dying, and all I had to do was just...

"Hey," she says. And suddenly I realize why I went through the whole bullet dodging dance all those times. I wanted to look like an action hero, not a crazy homeless time traveler or whatever the hell kind of crazy homeless person I am.

I look around; some of the customers are taking pictures of me with their cell phones, which isn't good. But at least she's fine.

"Hey!" she says again, this time a little louder and with a lot of alarm in her voice. I hold my hands up in the universal sign of submission. I'm not the bad guy here.

"Look out!" she yells.

I turn around in time to see Santo standing up. He's holding her ex-boyfriend's gun, checking to make sure there's still a round in the chamber.

"Yeah, so I forgot to tell you," he says.

Santo suddenly lifts the gun, and even though I know that bullet will go right through me and into whoever's on the other side, I instinctively move between him and Cady.

BAM! He fires at something behind me and to my left.

I turn in time to see Cady's worst nightmare, now the worst nightmare of everyone in this coffee shop, slump to the ground. Minus most of his head and all of his life. Everything he ever learned and believed and remembered and forgotten is now splattered all over the counter and wall. And all over all the blueberry muffins.

"I'm a Reset too," Santo finishes.

I look back and forth between him and the cadaver he made. "You didn't have to do that," is all I can think to say.

"Oh, come on, I'll buy you a better muffin."

I mentally set aside the fact that a better muffin does not exist in this or any parallel universe and bolt for the door. And I even make it outside.

# 9

I hit the sidewalk and turn to run in one direction only to see a cop car pulling up. So I turn to run the other way.

But there's a fate worse than Santo that's been looking for me, and I suddenly find myself face-to-face with all three hundred pounds of it. He's big and blonde like a Nazi wet dream, and he looks angrier than usual, probably because of that black eye he's sporting.

I'm not saying he looks angry because he has a black eye. I'm saying he looks angry because I gave it to him.

I turn to run back toward the cop, but fate grabs a fistful of my neck and hauls me in like a big evil kid hugging a raggedy little teddy bear.

"Let me guess," I say. "You just wanna talk?"

"You think I wanna talk?"

His name is Pete, by the way, but I used to call him re-Pete, right before he'd murder me. And I don't have to tell you where he got that nickname. Guy's a stunning conversationalist.

He's also stunningly top-heavy. Thing is, he could easily pick me up and carry me like a rag doll, he's done that many times before. But first, he'd have to shift his weight to avoid losing his balance.

Before he can do that, I lift my knees to my chest, forcing him to topple forward and triggering a reflex that makes him spread his arms out to break his fall. And just like that I'm free.

Well, sorta. I don't think I can outrun him. I'll need to slow him down first.

I turn around and try with all my might to cram my tibia up his vas deferens, but he turns and bends slightly like he's taking up a fighting stance. And my shin, instead of smashing into his soft, tiny balls, slams into his big hard knee instead.

All the nerves between my leg and ego scream as I struggle to remain standing. Suddenly incarceration isn't such a bad idea, I think to myself as I hobble and limp toward the cop.

"I did it! I killed that guy!" I shout while looking over my shoulder. Re-Pete doesn't look as unsure of himself as a human being should look right now, but I'm too busy trying to get arrested to pay any attention to him.

I follow the cop's orders, lying down on my stomach, turning my face away, spreading my arms out with the palms up and crossing my legs at the ankles. He kneels on my back, brings my wrists around, puts the bracelets on them, then sits me up.

"It's not him, he didn't do it!" Cady shouts as the cop leads me, still limping, to his car. A couple brave people from the coffee shop follow her out onto the sidewalk, still taking pictures on their cell phones. I shake my head at Cady but she keeps shouting. "You got the wrong guy! The guy you're looking for went out the back!"

Fortunately, the cop isn't paying attention to her. Or maybe he is and that's why he's hurrying me into the back seat of the cruiser. He doesn't even frisk me.

He hurries to the driver's seat, jumps in and turns the engine over. I lean forward and try to get his attention through the steel grate.

"Hey, I just want you to know I'm going to cooperate, OK?"

He ignores me, which I expected. The pain in my leg is wearing off but the hot, hollow feeling in my gut isn't going anywhere.

"Hey! Hey!" Cady's still on the sidewalk, standing next to re-Pete now, shouting at the cop. I can hear her through the windows and over the sound of the engine, her voice is going up in pitch. Whether it's from anger or fear, I can't tell. They both sound the same.

Then it occurs to me, it's weird that the engine is running. I figured he'd put me in the back seat and then start taking statements or something, but I didn't expect him to get in and start the car.

"Aren't you supposed to wait for the cavalry to show up?" I ask.

Cady looks around at her fellow coffee shoppers for moral support but they're still too terrified to be of any help. Then she looks at re-Pete and is suddenly so deeply unsettled at making eye contact with him that she takes a step back. It looks like an entire world passes between them in the space of a heartbeat, and that world eclipses everything she can think or say or feel or do.

And just like that it's over; re-Pete turns and looks at the cop, the cop gives him a curt little nod, and re-Pete waltzes away like nothing happened. The cop puts the car in reverse and starts backing away, fast.

That's when I know how truly fucked I am.

# 10

She's used to being treated like a non-person, so much that she doesn't even take it personally anymore. But there's something about the way he's objectifying her that makes her feel like she's in a falling elevator, and he's not even looking at her chest. Now, suddenly and for the first time in all her living memory, she wishes she could go back to the familiar comfort of being leered at without eye contact. And all this crosses her mind in less time than it took her to utter the word 'hey.'

That feeling is gone the instant he turns to the cop, nods, and calmly walks off like he has someplace else to be and isn't fleeing an active crime scene or something. Which is the last straw for Cady; she just watched her stalker die, she was saved by her handsome-but-scruffy coffee shop line buddy who seemed to remember her despite having never once made eye contact, then she watched him confess to a crime he didn't commit. Now he's being hauled away to who-knows-where, and no one seems to even notice much less care except for the big creepy gorilla who acted like he orchestrated the whole thing.

"Excuse me," says a voice next to her.

She turns to the older gentleman she held a door for just a few moments ago, back when the world still worked the way it was supposed to. He holds up his cell phone to show her something, and starts swiping through pictures of everything that just happened like her life is flashing before her eyes.

"I thought I was documenting my own death, you know, for the investigators," he explains while swiping past pictures of her, her stalker, and her savior. "But then I thought, I don't want to be the guy who takes pictures of his killer for his kids to see, so I stopped. But I did get a good one of, you know," he nods in the direction the cop went while swiping once more and landing on a picture of her rescuer. It's actually a really good shot.

"Can I get a copy of that?" she asks as she takes out her phone, and he nods, eager to share.

Someone once said that attachment is the root of all suffering. It's the kind of thing someone would say who's never been in the back of a cop car.

"You didn't read me my rights!" I scream as I kick the partition, the doors, the windows, anything and everything I can, but neither the cop nor the car are moved.

I should be conserving my energy. I should be paying attention to my surroundings so I can tell the cops where they took me. I should be asking this cop if I can borrow his phone to call the cops, but something tells me he won't let me.

We pull into a secluded park, past a heavily graffitied playground with a makeshift lean-to on one side. There's a homeless guy watching us from under the tarp.

A Town Car pulls up parallel to us, facing the other way. The cop gets out and opens my door just as the Town Car door opens, forming an enclosure of metal and fear. A familiar big body with a big black eye steps out of the car and reaches into my personal space. I kick at his hand, but he's as fast and angry as I am spent and tired. He catches me by the ankle, drags me across the enclosed space and props me up like a rag doll on the seat.

The interior of the Town Car is just gorgeous. Plush, hand-stitched leather everywhere, tinted windows, a minibar near the divider. And ashtrays. I wonder how much damage I could do in here before re-Pete manages to stop me. And then I wonder what kind of damage he'd do to stop me. I don't want to wake up and spend a forever of tomorrows in agony, so I just smile at the big piece of meat. It stares right back at me.

"I got my nose broken this morning," I say.

The smile disappears under his black eye. I can see the homeless guy getting out of his lean-to and running away out of the corner of my eye.

"But I'm all better now," I continue. "How's that shiner?"

"How's the shiner?" re-Pete asks. His fist reaches my face before the signal from my eyes can reach my brain. The pain burrowing up into my sinuses hits me next.

My hands cover the pulped mess through which I used to breathe. Blood oozes out between my fingers and onto my shirt, creating a masterpiece of modern art that perfectly reflects the underlying metaphor of how much it sucks to be me right now.

"It's getting better, thanks," he finishes, the smile creeping back up onto his big meaty face.

I swallow a big tug of blood and then start thrashing in my seat, trying my best to break something, anything, before re-Pete can restrain me.

But he's faster than me.

# 12

I spend the next twenty minutes or so feeling like I got shanghaied into a bondage show and probably looking even worse than I feel. Because I've got re-Pete's brown leather belt trussed around my ankles, and it really doesn't go with these silver handcuffs.

I couldn't check my phone or watch even if I had one, but I know this drive takes about twenty minutes at this time of day because once, in a previous life, I actually drove myself here.

And I can tell we've arrived from the look of grim determination on re-Pete's awful face. That and the fact that the car has stopped. That and the fact that re-Pete is taking the belt off my ankles. Like I'm going to just mosey on into hell with him.

"We can do this the easy way or the hard way," says re-Pete in a rare display of knowing how to borrow sentences from someone other than the person in front of him. It feels like I'm watching him evolve before my very eyes.

If you're wondering why I'm not panicking, it's not from knowing I've escaped this nightmare before. It's from thinking about how to get my body through the space between my arms so I can get my hands out in front of me. It's having something to focus on. Now if only he'll let me focus.

"Can you give me a minute?" I ask. "My legs are asleep."

"Your legs are asleep?"

Well, evolution is a slow process whether it's within an entire species or between a special person's ears, especially someone as meaty as re-Pete. It's not like I can expect him to move faster than...

Before I can finish that thought he reaches in, grabs me by the ankle, hauls me out of the car and throws me over his shoulder in one smooth, polished motion. I lost my focus. If I had my hands in front of me, I could rain blows down on his back. But that would probably just feel like regular rain to this big golem.

I squirm and buck like mad anyway as he carries me past muddy tire tracks toward the entrance. I catch a glimpse of a new construction project on the side of the building before I'm hauled through a set of sliding glass doors and past the reinforced steel gate behind them. There's an empty reception desk that never seems to have a receptionist behind it, and a closed lobby with two doors. One leads into a dormitory and office area. The other leads into a basement.

I know which one we're going through. Now it's time to panic.

I start thrashing around on his shoulder so hard he drops me.

Before he can pick me up again, I roll up onto my feet and run for the glass door to the lobby. But the motion sensor is off, so I come skidding to a stop in front of the doors.

My hands are still cuffed behind my back, so all I can do is kick the glass panels. But they're thick, they have a slight bluish tint around the edges, and the parking lot looks slightly mottled through them, which suggests they're made out of more than just layers of glass.

It's not clear whether they're bulletproof, but foot-proof they definitely are, and so apparently is re-Pete. I do manage to get a good kick in, but he still just picks me up again and hauls me back to that dreaded door.

I thrash around as hard as I can, enough to make him sidestep a couple times to keep his balance. But not enough to keep him from carrying me through the door and down the stairs. Down into a hallway lined with doors, each one a gate way into someone's personal hell.

Re-Pete throws me against the wall next to one of the doors and pulls my arms up so my shoulders are locked, forcing me to stand on my toes to get away from the pain.

My toes aren't long enough.

He unlocks the handcuffs then starts to unlock the door, so I turn to make one last stand. My right elbow arcs toward his left eye. It worked once before, he's still got the mark.

But he catches my arm this time, turns me around again, pushes the door open and then starts to push me through it. I get my legs up and plant a foot on either side of the door.

Re-Pete pushes, my boots scuffing the frame on either side until my legs collapse under me and I fall to the floor inside.

Then he slams the door shut behind me.

# 13

This room, like every other room in this hallway, is outfitted with a lock on the door, a tile floor, a drain in the center, and nothing else. There's no doorknob on the inside, no furniture, and no running water. These rooms don't need amenities. They just need to be hosed down every once in a while.

That door is the only exit; no amount of kicking or punching or pounding my head against the wall will get me out. This I know from experience.

And they're not going to open that door. This I know from logic.

Imagine you had an animal that came back every time you killed it. It'd be exhausting or terrifying, depending on how you felt about killing.

But now imagine you had an animal that didn't just come back, it went back. In time. To the moment it woke up to start the last day of its life. And now imagine it went back with all its memories intact, including the memory of how it had died. It wouldn't just know that you were going to kill it, it would remember how, and then eventually it would either escape or return the favor, depending on how it felt about killing.

And you wouldn't be able to stop it, because no matter how you planned on killing it, it would be ready for you, having already been killed that way once before. No amount of strength or skill would save you, you could have a gun or three black belts or be twice its size or all of the above and it wouldn't matter because that animal would adapt.

If you had such an animal, the only way to stay ahead of its learning curve would be by dying and going back with it. Or by locking it in a cage and never letting it out.

That's how I know they aren't going to open that door.

Because I am that animal.

# 14

She collapses the document on her monitor just as her boss rounds the corner and right before he can see what she's working on. Which makes it look like she isn't working on anything, which is worse than being caught wasting time on the company dime because instead of being angry, all he can feel is concern. And pity. And the weight of an unbalanced ledger; he's paying her by the hour, after all.

He forces a magnanimous smile onto his face, but it barely fits and they both know it. "You know, if you want to," he says.

"There's too much going on today, we've got," she cuts him off.

"Cady," he starts. But she freezes, her every muscle taut and tense; she's a tiger about to pounce on a tourist, not a housecat chasing dust devils. He sees this and adjusts his tone to something less assertive and more like pleading before continuing: "...you should be resting, you should be shopping, you should be calling a lawyer. You should be suing someone, and it's not like you don't have sick time saved up, you know you can count this as..." He trails off. He expected relief for relieving her from work, but she hasn't relaxed a bit. If anything, she's even more intense.

"I. Can. Work," she says.

He backs away slowly with his hands up, palms facing out. "OK," he says, trying to look confident. She rewards him with a tiny and very slow nod until he's out of sight.

Then she pulls the document back up. It's a picture of her rescuer from the coffee shop, but it fills up too much of the page. So she sizes it down a tad so it fills just the top two-thirds of the page, leaving room for some text below.

# 15

I'm awakened from a dream by a knock on the door. Or maybe I'm still dreaming. I have no clue how long I've been in here or how long I've been asleep. I don't know whether I've died yet, or if I have, how many times. All I know is I'm not dead right now.

In my dream, the walls were transparent and I could walk through them, but I didn't because I was afraid of what I might find on the other side. Which is hilarious, because I know what lies on the other side, and I'd resort to unspeakable acts of violence to get there.

There's another knock on the door. Now I know it's not a dream.

"Mr. Mulligan?" A timid voice on the other side knows my name.

I get up and stand away from the door as my mind races through all the different times they came for me. In the beginning, they held up a tablet with a number on the side facing away from me and asked if I knew what the number was. It was the number eight every time.

Then they killed me. Every time.

Dying got old real fast, so I tried ambushing the guy with the tablet. At first, that guy was Santo, and from the way he reacted, it was clear he was expecting a fight. Then after a while, Santo was replaced by re-Pete, and re-Pete was much, much worse. But one of those times, I was able to lure him into the room with me.

So I stand back and wait, trying to look as feeble and weak as possible. I won't even acknowledge the new guy until he crosses the threshold. Then it'll be time for those unspeakable acts of violence.

I can hear the click of a key being laid on the ground outside the door. It sounds like it's a mile and a million years away but I can still hear it over the hammering of my heart in my ears.

"Mr. Mulligan?" I'm trying to bait him inside; he's trying to bait me to the door. And baiting is waiting. I can wait harder.

"Mr. Mulligan, I assure you there's no need to pounce like a lion."

OK, I wasn't expecting that. The voice is not timid, that's not the right word.

It's weak.

I take a step forward before realizing I'm responding to the voice because I feel stronger than it sounds. That is some strong bait.

A key slides languorously through the crack under the door and comes to a scraping stop inches from my feet. My pulse in my ears sounds like jets crashing rhythmically into buildings but that key sliding across the tile floor is louder.

"Mr. Mulligan, you are free to go. When I told them to bring you here by any means necessary, I was referring to monetary means and not force. Please know that you have my sincerest apologies for what you have been through."

I wait for what feels like a minute and a hundred lifetimes. And I know what a hundred lifetimes feel like.

Then I hear a step and a click. Followed by a step and a click. And another. The sound of a cripple with a cane.

I snatch up the key and stand back to examine it. There are no markings on it, just like there are no markings on the door.

I fit it into the lock and turn it. The latch moves in and out. I open the door, just a crack, enough to know it works.

A key is a funny thing; you only need it when a door is locked, the rest of the time it just takes up space in your pocket. I feel like I should leave this thing in the room for the next Reset, but there's no place to hide it.

So I put the key in my pocket and then I put my fingers inside the crack of the door.

And then I slam it open.

# 16

A frail-looking older gentleman in a crisp but dated-looking suit stands at the other end of the hallway, opposite the stairwell. He's leaning on a cane, bathed in the glow of a red exit sign, and surrounded by darkness. The overhead fluorescent lights are off, so I'm guessing it must be night outside.

I step out of my room and the door clicks shut behind me. There's nothing between me and the stairwell to the lobby. My choices are an old man with a cane on one side and a way out on the other. A fight or a flight of stairs.

I don't know what lies up those stairs, and I don't want the old man at my back when I find out, so I turn to face him.

"Where's re-Pete?" I ask.

"I beg your pardon?"

"The gorilla. Is he in one of these rooms?" I look at the other doors, all of which are closed. The only way to tell which hell was mine is by the scuffmarks I left on the frame when re-Pete put me there.

"Ah, you mean Peter. I imagine he is asleep right now, although it is not my place to do more than imagine. He is, as you might say, 'off the clock' at the moment."

I look back toward the stairs. Something's not clicking here, and it's not just the subtle classism in that remark.

It's the fact that the only thing standing between us is about twenty feet of stale air.

"Do you know what I am?"

"I know quite a lot about you, Mr. Mulligan."

"Then why aren't you afraid?"

There's something about the way he smiles that makes him look more dangerous than re-Pete. "I should be, no? After everything you have been through, I should expect you to kill me without so much as a how-do-you-do. But you could have killed Peter once upon a time, and yet you only wounded him enough to get away."

"I won't make that mistake again."

"Irrelevant, Mr. Mulligan. As I said, you are free to go."

"As you said, with your sincerest apologies."

"Assuming you want nothing more?"

I want to punch you in your smug mouth, I almost say. But his mouth isn't as smug as the words falling out of it, and those words are right. I want nothing more than to get out of here.

So I turn and start doing the one-foot-in-front-of-the-other dance, knowing I'm going to spend the rest of my life wondering what the hell this was all about.

And then I'll probably spend the rest of the next life wondering as well, and the next one after that.

Which makes me wonder how many of these lives I have left, and what will happen when I run out. Or worse, what will happen when I don't. This might be the last chance I'll have to ask before finding out the hard way. I turn around with a question on the tip of my tongue, but before I can spit it out he blinds me with one of his own.

"Do you feel better?"

"What?"

"The program you signed up for..."

"I signed up for a depression study," I say, suddenly unable to contain the venom in my voice.

"Which is precisely why I must ask, Mr. Mulligan... Or may I call you Kenny?"

"How 'bout you call me a cab so I can run you over with it?"

He flashes that dangerous smile again. "Tell me Kenny, do you still suffer from an inexplicable need to die? Because in your current condition, that could become quite a habit."

"You think you did me a favor?" He's a better conversationalist than re-Pete, I'll give him that. But I came here to get cured, not killed.

"Au contraire, Kenny. My work would have been tremendously beneficial to you if I had accomplished what I set out to." He leans weakly against the wall and gestures toward the door behind him. "Unfortunately, I will likely now spend what remains of my life here, attempting to reverse the effects of what I assure you were the best of intentions."

I've been through enough to not care about his intentions, so I ask the only other question that comes to mind. "Who are you?"

"I am Dr. Ethan Prior, the founder of this facility." He gestures toward his door again, then down at his brittle-looking body. "As you can no doubt see, I've not a lot of time left with which to accomplish my work. And I can't imagine you might be interested in helping, now would you?"

I shake my head so hard I almost lose my balance. He straightens and steps away from the wall.

"Then I am afraid I must leave you to find your own way home, Kenny. Rest assured, if we do manage to find the cure, we will send someone to administer it to you." He turns and starts walking back down the hall, taking himself and all his knowledge away from me and the freedom that lies behind.

"Wait!" I shout. He turns. "What do you mean by 'cure?'"

"In order to understand a cure one must first understand the condition. And you have a very curious condition, Kenny. Unfortunately, I am afraid I haven't the time to chit-chat, as it were."

"That's it?"

He nods his head at the door behind him. "I have much to do. But if you'd like to follow me, I can answer your questions. You've earned that, at least."

I can't move. I can't decide. I can't even breathe.

He smiles sadly, then turns again to the door and walks through it.

I can get out of here right now. Assuming re-Pete isn't waiting to ambush me in the stairwell or lobby, I can waltz right out of here and spend the rest of forever living on the streets or picking up the pieces of my life while wondering whether a day will come when I'll stay dead and worrying about what will happen if I don't.

I don't want to spend the rest of forever wondering and worrying.

After a moment, I follow.

# 17

I step into another dim hallway filled with doors, one of which is open. I'm assuming that's where Prior lies waiting.

At least he wasn't waiting for me with some smug remark. No amount of love or money could have enticed me deeper into this pit, but no amount of love or money could buy the answers I'm looking for either, and I'm sure he knows that.

This adds another corridor to the amount of space between me and my freedom. I'm sure he knows that as well.

I walk past a couple doors like the ones in the hallway to hell, except these have small, wire mesh-reinforced windows like the kind you'd see in a school or barracks.

Peering inside the first one, there's a table, some chairs, a microwave and a fridge. So normal-looking it's almost surreal. I bet it even has a doorknob on the inside.

The next one is filled with row upon row of empty cages stacked one upon the other.

The third door is the open one, light flooding out into the hallway. I approach slowly to let my eyes adjust, then I step into what looks like a set from a low budget science fiction movie. There's a long, thick tube suspended on metal sawhorses running up and down the length of the room, dozens of computer monitors on either side, and hundreds, maybe even thousands of hard drives connected by more wire than my eyes can comprehend.

To one side of this technological catastrophe, the pièce de résistance: a pair of metal tables with arms extending out of each side, looking like a crucifix fucked an execution table and gave birth to twins.

And in the middle of all this sits Prior with his back to me, typing away at a keyboard. Next to the keyboard on the desk sits, of all things, an empty cage like one of the ones in the room I just passed.

"Ah, Kenny. So glad you decided to join me after all. Come, I have so much to show you."

The monitor in front of him is devoid of pictures, icons, apps and appeal, littered instead with a jumble of gibberish and punctuation that looks like an alien language.

He adds a finishing touch to whatever it is he's coding and turns around. "When you asked before whether I knew what you were, I said I know quite a lot about you, which was quite pointedly vague because a more thorough introduction to that reality would come across as poetic at best, and. Well. Kenny, allow me to introduce yourself to you."

He hits the return key and numbers start running down the screen so fast I can't catch them. I know I'm supposed to be impressed, but the way he's staring at those scrolling numbers like a musician at his own masterpiece is too distracting.

"We mapped your every neural pathway, your every memory and experience, everything you ever learned and everything you ever didn't. This is the digital sum of all that you are."

The interviews, the tests, Santo reassuring me while putting the electrodes on my scalp... I figured out this wasn't a depression study by the time he started killing me, but it never occurred to me that I was being recorded.

"Can you read that?" I ask.

"Not in the conventional sense as reading assumes intent in communication, and this transcription is more of a picture than an essay, as it were. Structurally speaking, however, your mind is startlingly similar to my own, such that I can indeed translate a few bits and pieces though a combination of neurochemical phonetics and inference." He presses a key and the scrolling slows to a crawl. "Here we see a series of emotional memories, clutched together not because they happened sequentially but rather because of how you felt when they occurred." He speeds it up and then slows it down again. "And here you had a singularly intense experience, possibly of a very traumatic event releasing copious amounts of acetylcholine..."

"Does it say when and where that happened?"

"Kenny, while this is a map of sorts, it is ordered neither spatially nor temporally but rather by emotion and habit. I can tell from patterns that you have the predictably pointless dispositions of kindness and depression, but, oddly enough, quite a lot more resilience than most who suffer from your condition. Tell me, do you remember how many times we conducted the memory test with you?"

"You mean how many times your employees killed me?"

"Yes."

"No."

"How fascinating." He gestures around the room. "In this reality, you were only in that room for three days." Then he hits a key and the scrolling on the monitor speeds up to a blur. "But in your reality, in which time is neither linear nor even, the experience occurred so many times you lost track. I wonder, what would we see if we were to re-record you right now?"

"What would happen if I were to strangle you right now?"

He actually smiles at this. Bad sign. "Such an astute question! But I do not expect you will understand the math in which the answer lies, and our past and conditional verb tenses are too limiting, we would need to devise an entirely new sort of past paradoxical tense in order to fully..."

"I mean would you wake up this morning remembering things before they happen?"

"Yes."

"So you're a Reset, like me."

"Kenny my boy, I am the original Reset! Although that is not what I set out to become." He gestures toward a chair in front of one of the nearby monitors. "Sit, allow me tell you a story."

I don't feel like sitting. I feel like someone just destroyed my life and then offered me an eternity in hell and a cup of tea as a consolation prize. And I'm more of a coffee guy. So I just stare at him.

"Very well," he says with a sigh that sounds like Einstein explaining algebra to an eight-year-old. "Remain standing if you must, but look around this room and picture in it a slightly younger me, a somewhat older computer, and a rodent. Then let us begin our story with that remarkable question which you, dear Kenny, so eloquently posited. What would happen if you were to strangle me right now?"

# 18

"If you were to strangle me right now, you wouldn't," he says as he brings up a file folder on the monitor in front of him. "Because while you would no doubt be successful in your asphyxiating endeavors, I would not go, as the Welsh poet put it, gentle into that good night, I would rather *went*. Or to borrow from a less lyrical analogy, I would not leave this body, I would *left*. And you, dear Kenny, would not succeed because you would not have awakened to the sound of my knocking at your door but rather to silence, one day closer to death as before, alone in a room without sustenance."

His hypnotic tone pairs with the implied threat like Champaign with a scab sandwich. I'm only here for answers, I remind myself as he clicks on one of the files and launches a video player app. It's frozen on the first frame, showing Prior sitting at this same desk. "How very fortunate for you that you are so very loathe to violence, Kenny, as this makes you one of few to whom I will explain this terrible technology." I realize with a start that the camera must have been right where I'm standing, because I'm looking at him in front of a monitor which contains a picture of him in front the same monitor like one of those funhouse mirror effects where the image replicates itself within itself indefinitely.

"Our tale begins as tales of discovery often do," he continues, "with a rodent bred to the sort of tasks that send animal rights activists into fits of litigiousness, along with a slightly more sprightly me, right here at this very same station." He presses play on the app, and the video version of him, looking just as creepy and decrepit as he does now, releases the latch on the cage.

A cute little lab rat comes out of the cage and sits next to the keyboard, awaiting a treat. Prior in the monitor pets the little animal for a moment, then picks up a tiny helmet with protruding wires which he presents to the camera with a flourish. "We commence now with test subject number one, test number one hundred and ninety-one," video Prior says to the camera. He fastens the tiny helmet to the rat's head. The rat patiently allows this, looking at him with puppy-like trust.

"As you now know," the Prior in front of me explains, "whenever I perish, I do not die in the plebeian sense but rather return to a previous point in actuality with knowledge enabling me to alter the course of events leading up to my demise." Video Prior takes a crouton from the breast pocket of his lab coat, holds it between both hands, then forms his hands into fists and holds them in front of the rat as live Prior continues to narrate. "I was experimenting with a rodent, as we scientific entrepreneurs are often wont to do. In this instance, I was attempting to teach the creature something it could not be reasonably expected to learn through conventional means." The rat goes back and forth between the two hands, unable to figure out which one contains the crouton.

"All previous attempts at quantum communication involved predicting a particle's spin by measuring the angular momentum of a corresponding particle. These efforts failed, I might surmise, because they focused on measuring rather than constructing the message." Prior opens the hand with the crouton, taunts the animal with it for a moment, then puts the snack back into his pocket before getting up. "Commencing Quantum Projection," video Prior says as he crosses the room, moving the camera to track his movements. The rat in the video tries to follow but is tethered to the table by the wires extending from its helmet.

Live Prior explains: "My efforts, on the other hand, were radical in that they entailed projecting information into an elsewhere the existence of which had not yet been empirically proven to exist, as it requires an expansion of our understanding beyond the standard model of quantum mechanics. I won't lecture you on the differences between the Copenhagen interpretation, objective collapse, and pilot wave theories. Suffice it to say, we know that ours is not the only reality in this universe. Which we know because, when you smash particles together at a high velocity, sometimes those particles exit our reality and sometimes new ones appear in their place."

Prior in the video presses a button on a panel on one end of the long tube suspended in the middle of the room, then returns to his workstation where he presses the return key. A crude image of a tiny brain on the monitor flows into the middle of what looks like two tiny eight-bit projectiles just as they collide in the middle of the screen.

"I managed to build a particle accelerator and had succeeded in sending charged protons into and out of this universe, which in theory means I had succeeded in opening a subatomic wormhole, although I am painfully aware that the theoretical nature of that assumption is precisely what made the experiment so radical. And precisely why the experiment failed, or so I thought at the time." After watching the monitor for a moment, video Prior takes the crouton back out of his pocket and again offers both closed fists to the rat.

"The rat, you see, was shown the location of a morsel of food on only one occasion. This particular breed needed to be shown a location three or more times in order to form the habit we call memory, so if it were to find the treat with fewer than three attempts, probability would suggest that a memory had been somehow successfully transmitted back into the animal's consciousness." The rat sniffs at both hands again, unable to guess. It looks up at him, curious and trusting as if waiting for him to open his hands again.

"I'll admit, I did not expect this experiment to succeed. Nevertheless, it was frustrating. I'd spent weeks devising and executing variations of this test to no avail, so I decided to terminate the experiment and the subject with it. And it was in that very moment that I saw my first glimmer of hope." In that moment, the rat starts panicking and tries to run away. But it's still tethered to the desk by the helmet and protruding wires, so it squeals and squeaks and tries to run in another direction, and another, and another while Prior stares at it in amazement.

"It was as though the rat knew it was going to die, which was perfectly improbable as it had no experiential means with which to predict its death. And I needn't tell you the number of times one can kill the average mammal." Video Prior takes a clipboard, puts a thick book on it to give it some weight, then lifts it over his head and smashes the terrified rat to death. When finished, he smiles at the bloody mess. "Finally, a satisfying outcome!"

"Why are you showing me this?" I interject.

He pauses the video. "Because, as the cliched adage aptly illustrates, one must destroy the egg in order to make the omelet. Indeed, I would need to demolish hundreds of these metaphorical eggs to demonstrate the viability of this experiment, so I purchased the services of a lab assistant, along with many more lab rats, and set about proving I could endow them with foresight of their dying through the particle accelerator." He clicks on another video, this one showing him standing next to Santo in the room with cages, each containing a single rat. They look into one cage. Prior tosses a coin, catches it, places it on his wrist, the rat just looks at him blankly. He looks at the coin on his wrist; it came up heads.

"It was a simple test of probability involving a coin toss and a certain subjective element of observation," he explains. Prior and Santo in the video step to the next cage and repeat the experiment, but this time the rat starts freaking out as soon as the coin toss stops. Prior looks at the coin on his wrist; it came up tails. He nods to Santo, who swiftly shoots the rat with a pellet gun. "As I'd hoped, I'd managed to prove with mathematical certainty that these animals knew they were going to die. However, I still could not imagine how exactly they knew this."

"What does any of this have to do with my condition?" I interrupt again.

"You followed me in here because you wanted answers, did you not?" he says as he selects another video from the file folder. "Would you want these answers edited? Would you be satisfied with an abridged version?"

"I'd be satisfied with a verbal version."

"Kenny. After all that you have been through, you deserve to see this. That is, if you can handle it. There is no harm in leaving if you cannot stomach science."

In other words, show me your strength by giving up and going along. I always thought it showed more strength to resist this sort of manipulation, and I shift my weight on my feet, ready to run the hell out of here and do exactly that. He sees this and adjusts his pitch.

"What you should be wondering is whether I can trust you enough to share proof of my own first felony," he says as he presses play on another video, this one of security camera footage from inside the lobby of the building. I hesitate, not because I want to gain his trust but because I'm planning on running out through that same lobby in just a few seconds and I hadn't even noticed the camera before. I want to see what it covers.

"I had sent my own neural map into the void hoping to gain some insight but was unwilling to conduct the rest of the test on myself. Fortunately, someone else was, although I did not feel so fortunate at the time." In the video, Prior enters a code into a security terminal just inside the smoky glass doors, then quickly steps through and waits for them to close behind him. Just as they do, a large, smiling man steps out of the shadows. And suddenly I can't help but watch, because I recognize the look on the second man's face. There's violence in his smile.

Prior looks to the side; the way is barred by another smiling thug. "While departing late one evening, I was set upon by a pair of unruly hoodlums. They demanded money, of which I had none, in exchange for my life, of which I had but one. Or so I believed."

He pauses the video just as the first thug produces a knife. And even though it's dark and I'm seeing the scene on grainy footage shot through tinted glass, I can see a glint on the blade. "I do not have footage of my death as that only exists in another reality, but suffice it to say, I came up short in that negotiation and closed my eyes one final time, only to open them a moment later in my own bed as if returning from a fitful dream. Now, I needn't describe the sensation of déjà vu that lasts an entire day, as you yourself have experienced this."

"I went about my day as before, and by the end of the day that I had adjusted to my new reality with a sense of elation for which words cannot suffice. Because while I did not understand this gift, much less how to describe it, it was enough to know that I had it and my assailants did not. And so as I departed that evening, I was prepared."

He presses play again; I can't see his face in the video, but I can see the pistol he takes out of his pocket. And I can see the smile on the thug's face turn to fear, just before Prior shoots him through the teeth. "You see, they killed me once without a morsel of remorse. Such is the nature of our woeful existence; here today, gone tomorrow, no hard feelings as it were. A hard lesson in life for anyone to learn, but they took the time to teach it to me and so it seemed only appropriate that I should return the favor."

He turns to the side and takes careful aim as the second thug runs out of the shot, then fires again. In the flash of the gunshot, his face lights up with a smile.

# 19

He turns and looks at me with that same smile. "What happened to the rats?" I ask, unable to disguise the fear in my voice. But from the look on face, he thinks he's hearing awe. Or admiration.

"Oh, we disposed of them. In this reality, they are very much past the point of decomposition."

"But in they still exist in another reality?"

"In a separate but infinitely repeating reality, if my math and our experience are any indication."

"But they're dying. Isn't there some way they can come back?"

He shakes his head and smiles sadly, but his sadness seems to be more for me than the rats. "This is difficult to explain precisely because of that past paradoxical verb tense we have yet to devise, as you are inquiring about an intersection between a future in their reality and a point in our past. Rest assured, they will not overwrite our reality because they have not already. To do so they would have had to learn to work together, and such is not in their nature."

I look around the room. I'm hungry and tired and terrified and none of that has anything to do with why I so desperately want to get the hell out of here.

"Where's the bathroom?" I ask as I edge toward the door.

"Kenny, there is so much more you need to know. About your condition."

"I'm just... I gotta..." I bolt out into the hallway only to stop short at the last thing I ever thought I'd encounter in this nightmare.

An elderly woman. With a transparent tube coming out of her face like ghost tendrils. The tube is attached to an oxygen tank on little wheels that she's dragging behind her with one hand. In her other hand, a metal cane with four prongs. She's trying to open the door to that surreal-looking room with the chairs and the fridge and the microwave, but her hands are full.

I go and get the door for her. Physically, she looks exhausted, but when she turns and smiles at me, her eyes are bright and full of life.

"You look like you need coffee more than I do," she says as she hands me the handle to the oxygen tank.

"I'm just... I gotta..."

"Hush now, you'll be right as rain in a minute or three."

I follow her into the kitchen, but only because I'm dragging a piece of metal filled with compressed gas that's attached to her face.

There's an olive-skinned twenty-something sitting at the table, his hair still wet and slicked back from a shower. He looks up from a stack of computer printouts in front of him. "Who's the new guy?" he asks.

"I'm just... I gotta," I say.

"Let's get him fed first and worry about pleasantries later," she says.

The young guy gets up and opens the freezer full of frozen microwave meals while the old woman bustles over to a cabinet full of mugs with me and the oxygen tank in tow. "All's we got breakfast-wise is like, eggs and sausage and shit," he says. "But there's this Indian spinach and cheese shit, and some French bread pizza shitty fucking shit."

"You really do swear too much," she tells him while pouring coffee into mugs.

"Well what else you gonna call microwave pizza made out of French bread? That's insulting even to French people!"

"You guys work here?" I ask.

"Ha! You wanna call it work," he answers nodding toward the papers on the table. "I'm Grazi. Guinea pig," he says offering me a hand which I impulsively take and shake. "Get it?"

"Hush, Grazi, let the man settle in before you assault him with your sense of humor. I'm Ellie. Cancer," she says while handing me a mug which I impulsively take and almost shake like another hand.

"Uh. Kenny. Sagittarius."

"No, I mean I have cancer."

"C'mon Ellie, we all do," Grazi says.

"Yes, but I had it before I got here," she explains. "I figure, I can't donate my organs and I've got nothing else to leave behind, so."

"Wait, what do you mean 'we all do?'" I ask.

"It is that curious condition to which I was attempting to elucidate you," says Prior, standing just inside the door. I guessed right, there is a knob on the inside.

"You were talking about cancer?" I ask.

"What, you didn't know?" Grazi asks me before turning to Prior. "How does he not know?"

"Kenny was a participant in a separate study," Prior explains before turning back to me. "Kenny, I am so very sorry, but this is what I have been trying to tell you. A side effect of this study is a particularly aggressive form of cancer. Had I known..."

"What happens when I die of cancer?"

"The same thing that happens when you die of anything else."

"I just, I reset? I'm just going to keep resetting and dying? Of cancer?"

"As I said before, if we do manage to find the cure, we will send someone to administer it to you."

"Wait, Kenny? You're leaving?" Ellie asks.

"The study in which Kenny participated was particularly taxing, and he is understandably exhausted," Prior says.

I set the coffee cup down and lean the oxygen tank against the table so it won't tear the tube out of Ellie's face. It's the least I can do.

It's all I can do to not tear through Prior like paper tape at a finish line. But he steps aside; no one stops me as I run out into the hallway. Then into the next corridor, touching the key in my pocket as I pass the scuffmarks on my own personal gateway to hell.

I don't meet death in the stairwell. It doesn't lie waiting in the lobby. Or in the parking lot. It isn't around the corner, or down the street, or in the next town over.

It's inside me.

I don't know how much time has passed before I'm aware that Prior is sitting next to me. I'm on the curb outside the front door, gazing at the hill on the other side of the parking lot, not so much wondering where I'll go next as whether I should even bother.

"The first time I died, I thought that everything I had ever accomplished in life was over," he says. "I could not imagine that it was just another beginning."

"How the hell is this a new beginning?"

"We are making considerable progress," he starts to reply before I cut him off.

"What, your lab rats graduated from croutons and single digits to differential equations?"

"I admire your sense of humor, Kenny, but I am being serious."

"So am I."

"Very well then, I would like to posit a serious question, if I may. Imagine that you have a lifetime of work to accomplish and only six months in which to do so. What course of action would you take?"

"I get it, and again, the answer is no."

"I am not asking you to help me," he says as he takes a gun out of his pocket. Instinctively, I almost go for it. But if I die, I'll wake up again wherever I woke up last, which means I'll wake up in that room, where I'll die of starvation instead of cancer. And it's not that I know which death will be better. It's that I don't.

I don't see any way out of this. And I don't see what's coming next, either.

He puts the gun to his head. "I learned something today, Kenny. I already knew that you could have killed Peter, once upon a time, but you did not. And today, I learned why. You are one of the astonishing few who cannot help himself but to help others. Now I could reset myself and go back to the beginning of the day, but would that bring me closer to my goal of accomplishing a lifetime of work in six months?"

He puts the gun back in his pocket when I don't answer. "No, because I also know that your willingness to help others is useless if you are not willing to help yourself." He gets up slowly, clearly in pain.

He starts to turn, then pauses. "On this floor, down the hallway to the left, there is a door with your name on it, with a bed, fresh clothes, and a private washroom. That and anything you can find to eat in the kitchen is yours, if you change your mind. If you do not change your mind, do not speak of anything you saw here to anyone, and wish me luck. We will find you once and if we ever do manage to find the cure."

And with that, he walks inside.

# 21

BAM! My eyes slam open at the sound of a muffled gunshot in the distance. Or maybe it was just a dream.

I look around expecting to see Meatball's ugly mug, but I'm not on cold asphalt in an alley, I'm in a bed. In what looks like a hotel room. With my name on the door. It was a hand-scrawled post-it note, but still. I felt welcome.

At first, I told myself I was just going to eat, shower, and then be on my merry way. Then I told myself I was just going to take a little nap. Then I went back into the kitchen and ate every last piece of French bread pizza I could lay my hands on. Grazi was right, it tasted like I was insulting French people with every bite. But while I'm used to better food, no amount of gourmet dumpster dining will ever beat a warm meal in a clean kitchen.

I try and tell myself that's not why I'm still here.

The alarm clock on the nightstand says 4:15. I walk out into the dark lobby and down the stairs into the hallway to hell, passing the door with the scuffmarks on the frame. I'm still almost swept away in a wave of emotion when I see that door, but not with the familiar fear of dying. It's more like a fear of acceptance.

I step into the kitchen to find Ellie standing in front of the coffee pot, her back to me. So I start to back out.

"I'm making some for you too," she says. There are two mugs on the counter next to the coffeemaker.

"Sorry, it's uh. It's me. Kenny."

"I know who it is, hon. Ethan told us you were staying." She turns around and regards me. "Oh, and you do clean up well, look at you."

I step back into the kitchen as she pours coffee into the two mugs.

"Someone once told me they have coffee in hell but you can't drink it," she continues as she sets the mugs down on the table. She slowly takes a seat, then picks one of the mugs up again and inhales the vapor, smiling. "I figure as long as I can smell it, that's heaven enough."

I plant myself in the chair next to her and take a thoughtful sip. "When did Ethan say I was staying?" I ask.

"Oh, sometimes he knows people better than they know themselves," she says, shaking her head. "And other times he can be clueless to the point where I start to doubt his humanity. You know how long it took to get him to buy us coffee? We were literally dying for it!"

She laughs silently at her joke, then asks "So where were you deployed? If you don't mind me asking."

"How did you know I was in the service?"

"I've seen those on uniforms before," she says, pointing to the tattoo on my arm. "And I've seen a lot of those, too," she says, pointing at my yes. "One tells me what kind of unit you were in. The other tells me it was a line company."

The tattoo she pointed at is something I don't even look at anymore. Not because I'm used to it, I just don't like looking at the thing. If I were to develop a cancerous mole next to it, I probably wouldn't notice until too late. "Not a lot of people know that term," I say.

"And the ones who do don't talk much," she answers. "My husband, when he came home from the war, he grew a beard, drank, bought a motorcycle, all the things veterans do to forget. And none of the things that actually help, like talking about their experiences."

"That's because it's all like disconnected scenes from a hundred different horror movies," I begin. "Like I was patching up a soldier with a head injury. I was in the same convoy when the I.E.D. went off, it could have happened to me, and it felt like it was happening to me because this guy was like my brother. And I had him under control. Perfusion was good, no internal bleeding. I was going to send him home with a purple heart and a matching scar. I mean, it was just a head wound! But then his head exploded. I was sitting there holding him in my arms, and they shot him through the head."

I drain the coffee in my cup. It's dark, bitter, and it burns, just like the memory. I get up and refill my cup, then sit down and just stare into the blackness.

"Do you feel guilty about it?" she asks after a while.

"I didn't do anything. I didn't even pick up my rifle, I figure they'll kill a man down, they'll kill me before I can do anything about it. But they didn't. They knew."

"What did they know?"

"You don't have to kill a man who's already dead on the inside."

"Ah. But there's something they didn't know."

"Oh yeah, what's that?"

"That there are ways to change people besides killing them," she says.

"Yeah. I'm sorry. You were married to a veteran, I'm sure you've heard a lot of these stories."

"Not really, no. But only because I was too busy trying to fix him to let him tell me what needed fixing."

"What happened to him?"

"Oh, he got better, don't you fret. We learn from our experiences. He just needed time to learn from his. As did I."

I look at the tattoo on my arm. There's no cancer that I can see.

"Did Prior tell you about the rats?" I ask.

"Yes."

"How do you know he doesn't see you as just another lab rat?"

"Trust in human nature, I guess."

"You trust him?"

She puts her hand reassuringly on mine. "Trusting in human nature doesn't mean trusting in the nature of a single human. Think about it this way, Kenny. The same energy that wiped out Hiroshima powers homes nowadays. That's because every time someone figures out how to make a weapon, someone else figures out how to turn that weapon around."

# 22

The alarm clock on the nightstand says 9:45. I've been lying in this bed for hours now, unable to get back to sleep.

I walk into the lobby, now filled with light, and continue down the stairs and past the door with the scuffmarks. I feel like I'm about to step into a pool of boiling gasoline with a lit cigarette in my mouth. The fear is back. Can't believe I'm doing this.

I continue through the next corridor and into Prior's enormous lab, only to stop short when I see what looks like a wall of meat in a lab coat standing with its back to me.

"Ah, Kenny, so good of you to join us," Prior says next to the meat wall. Last time I saw that big ugly thing, it was using my boots as brushes to paint scuffmarks on a door frame before throwing me through that door into a cold corner of hell.

Prior looks back and forth between me and re-Pete, then snaps his fingers. "Peter," he says. "We have a guest. And I think we owe our guest the courtesy of a customary greeting, do we not?"

Re-Pete finally turns around and fixes me with an empty stare. "Do we?" he asks before answering himself. "Yes, we do. Hello, Mr. Mulligan."

"Very good. And is there something else we owe him, Peter?" Prior asks.

"Is there something else? Yes, an apology. I'm sorry, Mr. Mulligan."

"There now, isn't it amazing how a simple and sincere statement of contrition can clear up an unfortunate misunderstanding between two dedicated colleagues? Kenny, I hope you feel better?"

I feel like my feet are nailed to the floor. Even as re-Pete turns back to his computer monitor, I can't stop staring at him.

"Now, if I may fill you in on our program and progress thus far?" Prior asks, gesturing at the monitor in front of re-Pete.

From where I'm standing, all I can see are columns of numbers, not entirely unlike the stream of code that turned out to be me. But I realize Prior's waiting for me to respond, so I nod.

"As we no longer recruit new participants, Grazi and Ellie now spend their days memorizing the results of our tests before taking a temporal shortcut with those data. An extraordinarily unglamorous endeavor, as most of their labor incorporates rote memorization of what must appear to them to be nothing more than meaningless mathematics. How fortunate that you, Kenny, have been selected for an assignment that is simultaneously simpler and substantially more rewarding."

As I stare at the monitor while Prior drones on, I realize numbers actually don't look like the scrolling code that Prior described as the sum of all that I am. These look like peoples' initials followed by numbers and dollar signs. Like a ledger of some sort. But again, he's waiting for me to respond, so I nod.

Prior continues on that cue. "A man of greater literary talent than I shall ever possess once said that necessity is the mother of invention. Would that I could hire such a wordsmith to design the verbal architecture for the plum assignment that you've been so lucky to land vis a vis our particular necessity, namely that of keeping the lights on, as it were. Peter, have we anything of sufficient significance today?"

"Have we?" re-Pete asks while pointing at one of the numbers. "Yes, we have." He points at the initials LGF, which are followed by a glowing green 4129%.That's when I get the pitch. The letters on the monitor don't represent people, but companies. And the one he's pointing at is a company that's just gone up in value like a newly outlawed drug.

"Ah, quite fortuitous indeed. What it would be like to be a stockbroker on Wall Street with the ability to go back in time and place an order at the start of the day just prior to a windfall of such violent proportions. But we needn't imagine..."

"Wait," I interrupt. "This is my plum assignment? You want me to die so I can report movement in the stock market?"

"Kenny, we are all engaged in dying," Prior says. "Would you rather be tasked with the memorization of something more complex?"

"No, I mean, why aren't you sending him back for this?" I ask while pointing at Re-Pete, who's glaring at me now.

"Do you doubt that Peter is one of us, Kenny?"

"No, I..." I'm frozen like a deer in headlights and it isn't from the murderous look in re-Pete's eyes. It's something in Prior's tone of voice. I can't put my finger on it, but it reminds me of the way he smiled when I asked what would happen if I were to strangle him.

"Perhaps a little test might be in order, hmm? Tell me Kenny, what time did you awake this morning?" Something in the way he asks this question suddenly makes me feel as confused as I am afraid.

"Uh, just now. Just a minute ago," I say. Re-Pete cocks his head at me like he knows I'm lying, but he doesn't say anything.

And Prior doesn't notice anything as he picks up a tablet and touches an app. "This is a random number generator, the same program we used in the earlier stages of human testing. It's set to single digits because I felt that the stress of dying would make it difficult for a subject to remember anything more complex."

He presses a button which sets a big wheel on the app spinning with a clicking sound effect. "Kenny, in a moment, you are going to press this button, which will select a number which neither Peter nor myself will be able to guess because you are not going to show it to us." The wheel stops spinning, landing on the number 8. My lucky number.

Prior hands me the tablet then walks over to re-Pete while taking a gun out of his lab coat pocket. Which he then points right at re-Pete's temple. A bead of sweat breaks out on re-Pete's brow as he towers over Prior. His life and what little that lies between those cauliflower ears now rests on Prior's trigger finger.

“Kenny, when you are ready, please spin the wheel,” Prior says. Looking at the tablet, that gun might as well be in my hand.

“Kenny, spin the wheel please.” My finger hovers over the button. I want to just pretend to press it, but I know he’ll know. Maybe I can replicate that clicking sound with my tongue.

“Kenny! Spin the wheel!” Prior shouts. I look up to see re-Pete’s big meaty face has gone completely white. There’s a single, tiny bead of sweat hanging ponderously from the tip of his nose.

I press the button and it rewards me with a loud click.

Except instead of spinning a large wheel full of numbers, a smaller wheel full of colors appears and starts to spin over it.

“Excellent, now, Kenny, in a moment, that wheel will land on a number. If Peter does not know which number it is, I will reset him. If he does know the number, that will tell us he’s already been reset today. Has the wheel stopped spinning, Kenny?”

The wheel never started. The app is still stuck on the number eight.

"Kenny" Has the wheel stopped spinning?" Prior asks.

I don't know what to say. It's still frozen. And re-Pete is almost drenched with sweat now.

"Kenny," Prior says in a softer tone without taking his eyes off re-Pete. "I understand being on either side of the gun is difficult. But you can rest assured knowing that Peter will know that number. You see, most people fear death merely because they have yet to experience it. But Peter here is one of us. Isn't that right, Peter?"

From looking at him, if I didn't know any better, I wouldn't think re-Pete was afraid of dying. I'd think he was afraid of death.

"There is a number on that tablet that only Kenny can see, Peter," Prior says. "What is that number?"

"Zero," re-Pete says without parroting the question.

"Is that the correct number, Kenny?" Prior asks.

"Yes," I lie. The app is still frozen.

Prior lowers the gun, hands it to re-Pete butt-first, then turns to me. "Now, Kenny, I have a choice for you to make. Earn your place on this team by earning our keep, or leave. What will it be?"

I'm just staring at the tablet, stunned and ashamed. The app is still frozen.

"Kenny? What will it be?"

Only when re-Pete takes the tablet out of my hand do I realize he's crossed the room.

"OK but not by him," I blurt out while stepping back from the big man. Who glances at the app and then back up at me with a look in his eyes I can't even begin to understand.

"Very well then, Peter, give me the gun. Kenny, you need but remember two things. The stock symbol LGF. And the time the stock went up, which was approximately 9:50 AM."

"LGF, 9:50," I say as re-Pete hands Prior the gun.

"One more time. Let us not waste this trip."

"LGF, 9:50," I say.

"Bon voyage, dear Kenny," Prior says as he raises the gun and points it between my eyes.

# 23

BAM! My eyes slam open at the sound of a muffled gunshot in the distance. Or maybe that's just my imagination.

I walk out into the dark lobby and down those dreaded stairs into the hallway to hell, passing the door with the scuffmarks on the frame. Another new wave of emotion hits me; this time, I just want to lock myself inside that room.

I trudge on instead to the kitchen where Ellie is standing in front of the coffeemaker with her back to me. "I'm making some for you too," she says.

"I know."

She turns around and looks at me, one eyebrow cocked like a loaded gun. "I've seen that look. You already know what's going to be said next, and not because you're going to be the one saying it."

"If you can smell the coffee in hell it'll still be heaven, your husband is a veteran," I start to say before she cuts me off.

"How's the coffee then, did I make it right?" she asks as she pours out two mugs.

"I'm back for more, aren't I?"

She puts the mugs on the table, takes a seat, then takes a sip. Then she sets it down and hits me with that loaded eyebrow again. "What would you like to know?"

"The work that Prior has you and Grazi doing. Do you know what it's for?"

"That's it?" she asks. "I've lived three times as long as you, through technological revolutions and major wars, I've seen dictators rise and fall, I can't even keep track of all the countries that have changed names since I first laid eyes on a map, and you're asking me about my day job?"

"Uh," is all I can think to say.

"Just kidding. Ethan says it has something to do with how far back we go. But so far, if I wake up at three o'clock, I go back to three o'clock. And I'm the only one here who wakes up before Ethan does. But that's all I know."

"You've been up since three?"

"Yes."

"Does Prior always ask what time you woke up?"

"Yes."

"Do you tell him you've been up since three?"

She slowly shakes her head and takes a sip to hide her smile.

# 24

I walk back up into the lobby feeling glad. And caffeinated. And hungry. We're all out of frozen microwave French bread pizzas, which is just as well because I could really go for a blueberry muffin right now.

I walk past the reception desk, which is devoid of reception as usual, to stand in front of the motion sensor. And lo and behold, the smoky glass doors part for me.

I run out into the parking lot before the doors can change their mind, then up to the street where I hang a left.

Rush hour isn't even in full swing yet, but the street is already crawling with commuters angrily tethered to their cars by seat belts and lease agreements. One guy in a particularly expensive-looking late model tries really hard to hide that he's checking me out when I meet his eyes. He was probably thinking about how fast he could go from zero to sixty if he weren't stuck in a sea of steel and chrome before I came along to give him his there-but-go-I moment.

Funny how I feel bad for him because he's stuck in traffic while he probably feels bad for me because I'm not.

It takes me about forty minutes to get to my favorite part of town, and I know I probably passed a hundred cafes along the way. But I also know what I'm craving and where to get it.

I pass the alley where I met Meatball half a dozen times in my reality, once in his, but he's nowhere to be seen. Maybe he got tired of Italian meatballs and found a dumpster behind a Swedish restaurant somewhere.

I cross the street, walk up the adjacent alley and emerge into a world of winners, all hurrying to punch a clock so they can win a little more. I recognize the car that passed me forty minutes or so ago with the guy who was trying hard not to be seen seeing me. It looks like he landed a really good parking spot, good for him.

Then I notice something next to the car, on the utility pole.

It's a picture of me. Taken in the coffee shop, the day I saved Cady. Above the picture, in large, bold font, the question: "have you seen this man?" And below it, a phone number on a bunch of tear-off tabs, none of which have been torn off.

I take the first one and slip it into my pocket.

"Hey kid, wanna buy a muffin?" asks a familiar voice behind me.

I turn around to get Santo in my peripheral vision while looking for an opening in traffic. But opening or not, I'm ready to run as soon as he makes a move. Best case scenario, I get away. Worst case scenario, I get run over. Going for a ride with this guy is not even a scenario.

But he stands at a respectable distance, his hands out and visible. He's holding a folded piece of paper in one of them.

"Man, are you popular right now. The cops are looking for you, except for one cop who claims he never saw you; he's on administrative leave. And the girl?"

He points at the utility pole behind me like I haven't already seen my picture on it. I don't take my eyes off him.

"She's looking too, and I gotta be honest," he continues, "I didn't think I'd beat her to you."

"You killed her boyfriend," I say. "Aren't they looking for you too?"

"Nah, see first of all, blaming me for his death is like blaming a banana 'cause you slipped on the peel. Not my fault the guy didn't know enough to stay down. Second? Everyone was getting pictures of you because they were getting pictures of the girl. You just happened to be in the frame. I'm lucky she's a looker. You, maybe not so much."

"I'm not going anywhere with you."

"Then we don't have a problem, because I'm not asking you to go anywhere with me."

"Then what do you want?"

"I want you to know what I know." He drops the piece of paper on the ground then slowly backs away from it. "Instead of some lie, because it's easier to accept."

With that, he turns around and walks away. I wait till he's out of sight, and then I wait until the bystanders who took in this whole interaction are gone as well.

And then I snatch up the piece of paper and run.

# 25

Elevator doors open into a plush office and out walks Cady with two cups of coffee in her hands, a bruised cheek on her face and a world of doubt in her eyes. She ignores coworkers who just stare at her by way of greeting as she makes her way past cubicles to the other side of the room.

She enters a corner office and sets the cups down on a desk in front of a lean middle-aged man wearing a thousand-dollar suit and a complementary fake tan. Behind him are floor-to-ceiling windows with a fantastic view of the bustling street below.

"You're late," he says.

"You're welcome," she says back.

"Did they catch the guy?"

"You mean the guy who gave me this?" she asks, pointing at her bruised face. "He was too dead to run when the cops showed up."

"Cady, if you need some more time, you know Bob can cover for you."

"No, that's. I just." She looks over his shoulder at the street below where Kenny and Santo are having their exchange. "Thanks I gotta go!" she shouts over her shoulder as she runs out of the office and back through the main room.

"Bob, cover for me, will you, thanks!" she finishes as she blows past one of her staring coworkers.

She runs past the elevator and into the stairwell, through the lobby and out into the street, scanning everywhere, looking for Kenny.

But he's already gone.

# 26

I hang a right back into the parking lot and march straight up to those smoky glass doors to stand in front of the motion sensor. But the doors don't budge. Even as I'm pounding on them.

Re-Pete emerges from the stairwell and walks slowly toward the doors to trip the motion sensor. Then he just stands there, looking at me funny like I'm supposed to know they only open from the inside.

It only occurs to me as I'm brushing past him that maybe this isn't my best idea ever. I wonder for just a moment whether I'm the person in the abusive relationship who only comes back because they think they can leave. But that thought competes with and loses to an overriding sense of self-righteous indignation as I run down the stairs, past the door with the scuffmarks, and right into Prior's lab.

"Kenny, where did you," he starts to ask.

I toss Santo's folded piece of paper onto his desk, cutting him off. He unfolds it and holds it up for me to see without looking at it himself. He already knows what it is.

It's a flier for a depression study, very much like the one that led me here. Same phone number and everything.

"Where did you get this?" he asks.

"I thought you said you weren't recruiting anymore!" I say, beside myself with fury.

"We are not recruiting anymore. This is an old advertisement. Who gave it to you?"

"So what happens when someone new calls that number, you just turn them away?"

"Obviously I am not going to inflict cancer on anyone else, knowing what we know now. Speaking of what we know now, we had some work to do today, did we not?"

I point to the monitor. "ELF. 9:50. Four thousand percent," I say.

He scrambles over to the monitor and scrolls through the stock symbols.

"That's fantastic, that's excellent, that's... Kenny. There is no ELF."

Shit. "There's gotta be. Maybe it's LEF, look under 'L.' Any of those at thirty-one-something right now?" The clock says 9:49.

Prior slams his hand on the desk, causing everything to shake, including me. "Kenny, I do not think you appreciate how many companies start with the letter 'L!'"

Just then, one of the symbols starts flashing as a line next to it spikes. I lean in to see what it was. LGF. Of course.

Prior opens a news feed as it continues to rise. "Speculation of corporate inversion. That was quite a lot of money to be made, Kenny. Where did you go this morning?"

"I thought you said I was free to leave."

Prior turns as the stock price finally starts to plateau. "You are indeed free to leave but you may not be free to return, or to participate in the benefits of this program, so I will ask you once again. Where did you go this morning?"

"To a coffee shop downtown."

"And did you perhaps meet with a former associate of mine at said coffee shop? Downtown?"

"Not unless your former associate is a blueberry muffin," I say.

Prior snaps his fingers and points at me. And next thing I know, I'm on the floor and re-Pete is going through my pockets. He takes out the slip of paper with the phone number on it and hands it to Prior.

Prior looks at it for a moment. "If I call this number, will I hear a familiar voice?"

"I hope not."

"Kenny, I do not think you fully appreciate the predicament you are in. Set aside the reality that there is nowhere you can go beyond my reach, and ponder, if you will, the fact that I have not gone after the person who gave you this," he says as he picks up the flier. "And do you not wonder why that is? Should I not be concerned that a former associate of mine is out there with a literal wealth of information that could be used against me?"

My shoulders rise in a shrug and then stay there as I shrink into myself.

"I am not concerned because I have neither the time nor the necessity to be so. Because this former associate of mine is going to die very soon, and not just once, not a thousand times, or even any ordinal number of times. Soon enough, he will wake up to see the last new day he will ever know. And then he will die and awake only to die again a number of times that can only be described with something that is technically not even a number. Not even I can begin to comprehend what that will be like."

He lets that sink in for a bit, as if it hadn't already, then nods at re-Pete who gets off me.

I get up.

"And as with my former associate, I have neither the time nor the need to look after you, Kenny, so I am going to ask you this one more time and one time only. Where did you go this morning?"

"To a coffee shop downtown. I swear. They have the most amazing blueberry muffins."

"Peter, do you know of this coffee shop downtown?"

"Do I know of it?" re-Pete asks. "Yes."

"And do they sell a blueberry muffin worthy of an eternity in agony?" Prior asks.

"I wouldn't know," he says. As if he'd even know what a blueberry muffin tastes like. The guy looks like he eats kids, not carbs.

"Kenny, would you like to remain a member of this team, participate in our research, and reap the benefits thereof?" Prior asks.

"Yes," I say without really considering the question. Something about re-Pete not repeating the last question is throwing me off.

"Then I need to know I can trust you, Kenny. In order to earn my trust, you must do three things. Remember the stock symbol LGF. Remember the time the stock went up, which was approximately 9:50 AM. And the third thing, of course: you must die."

"LGF, 9:50," I say as re-Pete unholsters the gun. I don't bother asking to be killed by someone other than re-Pete this time.

"One more time. Let us not waste this trip."

"LGF, 9:50," I say.

"And now for that third thing. Report to me as soon as you wake up," Prior says.

I can't see or hear re-Pete raising the gun behind me. I don't have to.

# 27

BAM! My eyes slam open. There's something about waking up after dying violently that I'm just not used to.

I run out into the dark lobby and down those dreaded stairs into the hallway to hell, passing the door with the scuffmarks on the frame. Another new wave of emotion hits me but I can't think of a word for it through all the anger I'm feeling.

I walk into the kitchen to find Ellie standing there as usual, her back to me.

"How many of us are there?" I ask. "Resets, I mean."

She pours out two mugs before answering. "Well, good morning to you too."

"If you can smell the coffee in hell it's heaven enough, your husband was a veteran," I start to say.

"You know they're called pleasantries for a reason?" she says while putting the two mugs on the table. "What?" she asks when I smile.

"Sorry, that just reminded me. I met this guy once, told me I could stand to learn some people skills."

"Hmm, reminds me of a man I know who once said he could get anything from anyone, because he had people skills. So we made a little bet."

"Did it have something to do with a meatball sandwich?"

She was just about to take a sip but puts her mug down instead, a tear forming in the corner of her eye. "How is he?"

"I didn't ask," I say as if I'd even notice. "He seemed happy."

"Of course he was happy. You could stick his head in a blender and the only thing he'd want in this world would be to fix the part of you that wants to sticks peoples' heads in blenders. It took me so long to understand that."

"Understand what?"

"How someone could be so happy and selfless at the same time."

With the blink of an eye, that single tear takes off on a short journey predestined by gravity to fall into her cup of coffee. It's so quiet in here I can hear the tiny plink.

After a moment, I ask: "Is it just you and Grazi here?"

"There were more of us," she says as she lifts the cup to her lips, but she pauses before sipping. "We'd wake up, memorize data, reset, and repeat. Not every day, mind you, but enough to make us relish growing a day older, if only for the sake of variety at the breakfast table. But every once in a while, we'd wake up and someone would be missing. I was under the impression everybody was quitting, because one-by-one, they all just disappear."

# 28

I walk back out into the dark hallway wondering what to do next when I notice the exit sign flickering. Odd that there would be a power surge at this hour.

That's when I notice the light in Prior's lab is on. I can't help but wonder why I hadn't noticed this before.

Peering in through the wire mesh window, there isn't much to see from this angle. But it looks like someone is on one of those T-shaped tables. In fact it looks like someone is on both of them. And I've been dying to know what those tables were for.

So I open the door, just a crack to see better, and that's when I'm caught.

"Kenny, had I known you were up this early," Prior says from one of the tables. He sits up and starts taking electrodes off his scalp.

I step inside to see Grazi strapped to the other table, and looking a bit out of it. Re-Pete stands behind Grazi's table looking like he doesn't know what to do with himself.

"Hello," I say to Prior. "Hey Grazi," I say to the only other intelligent person in the room, but he just stares back at me blankly.

"I'm sorry to interrupt," I start to say.

"No, Kenny, I'm glad you saw this," Prior says as re-Pete helps him get down from the table. "This actually is an experiment in which I hope you will be able to lend some assistance soon."

Takes me a moment but I manage to peel my eyes off Grazi. "Mind if I ask something?" I ask.

"Of course you may ask away to your heart's content," Prior says as re-Pete hands him his cane. "And I will happily answer away in return, as we are making considerable progress."

"By testing on yourself?"

"I wouldn't dream of testing on anyone else," he says as he moves to the side. This gives me a clear view of Grazi, who really looks out of it.

It also gives re-Pete a clear view of me.

"You went from trying to develop a communication technology to inventing time travel. Who are you going to sell it to?" I ask. Re-Pete starts to move toward the monitors along the wall next to me, and I step out of his way to let him. And to step out of his way.

"Such an astute question, Kenny. Some of our greatest technologies were initially developed for communication. Why, even the humble microwave oven came about when a man working on a communications device employing microwave radiation stepped in front of his contraption and noticed that it melted a chocolate bar in his pocket."

"He wasn't developing communication technology, he was developing combat radar equipment for the military."

"Ah, you are familiar with this story. As a former military professional yourself, I am sure you can appreciate the occasionally accidental and often quite surprising military applications that can come out of a research program such as this."

As a former military professional, I'm not sure 'appreciate' is the right word here. "Anyway, LGF, 9:50. Four thousand percent."

"I beg pardon?" Prior asks.

I point at the monitor with the stock symbols and am about to repeat myself, but I just realized re-Pete has stationed himself between me and the door.

"Oh, this is excellent news!" Prior exclaims as he rushes over to the monitor. "Kenny, great work! I believe a celebration is in order! Peter, do we still have any Champaign?"

"Yeah, thanks but I was thinking of getting a blueberry muffin," I say while looking around the room. The door's blocked, and re-Pete doesn't look like he's moving to get any Champaign.

"Kenny, but we have so much work yet to accomplish."

"I thought you said I was free to leave."

His eyes narrow. "Why are you so anxious to go? You wouldn't happen to be meeting with someone, would you?"

I look over my shoulder to see re-Pete in position, towering over me, and it's intimidating enough to make me hunch my shoulders and cringe. I cringe so hard and far my hands almost touch the ground.

And then, just as he reaches to grab me, I go those extra couple inches, planting my hands on the ground and donkey-kicking backward right into re-Pete's solar plexus.

His ass slams back into the wall while I stand up and turn around to shower him with punches and kicks. Which I'm doing in part to stun him, and in part to give myself a head start. But also in part to give myself a means of transportation.

I rifle his pockets, feeling around huge lumps of muscle as he looks at me through confused, glassy eyes. I probably only have a second or two, but I know it's enough when I find a set of keys with a car alarm fob on them. And a cell phone, which I figure I might as well take. Maybe I can score some gas money too, if one of these other lumps happens to be a wallet.

But out of the corner of my eye I can see Prior taking his gun off the table next to Grazi. Guess I'll have to worry about gas money later.

I vault over re-Pete and race out into the hallway just as a loud BANG goes off behind me. I make it to the end of the hallway and am through the door just as another shot goes off, but I'm still running, not suddenly waking up in a bed or next to a dumpster or in a cold room with a drain in the center. I make it up the stairs, through the lobby and into the parking lot.

Only then do I stop to check myself. I'm unventilated. No holes, no blood, no quick death rushing up to meet me. Just the same old slow one that looms in the distance for everybody.

I hit the unlock button on re-Pete's key fob and am rewarded with a flashing set of LED brake lights. "You have got to be kidding me," I mutter to myself. Re-Pete's ride is a tiny little piece of econo-crap that looks like some kid slapped a couple bicycles together to make a pretend car. Definitely not the big black limo he commands while on company business.

No time to look for a better option though, so I hop in, turn the engine over and transfer all my fear and anger as violently as I can through my foot into the pedal. After a moment, the little glorified golf cart starts to accelerate, if accelerate is even the right word.

# 29

I zip out of the parking lot and merge into a river of chrome and passive aggression. Rush hour. That magical place in space and time where people from all walks of life gather together to cut each other off in traffic so they can get a better parking spot somewhere.

Sometimes it's hard to tell where the person ends and the parking lot begins, like with the wannabe lumberjack who's screaming at the day laborers about how close they parked their pickup truck to his eco-friendly hybrid. Or the lawyer threatening the meter maid who's writing him a ticket for being an inch over an imaginary line. Or the artist in the vintage jeans and t-shirt ensemble pretending to take a call so he can ignore the panhandler with the matching outfit. The sort of scenery I used to see every weekday morning while inching toward my own destination, which, in hindsight, I realize was never so much a destination as a distraction.

There are a lot of things I miss about the rat race, but watching people compete for nothing through the frame of a car window is not one of them.

I signal a lane change only for the person in my blind spot to speed up, boxing me out. So I lean on the horn and merge into the lane with him, forcing him to choose between hitting his brakes or the right-rear butt cheek of re-Pete's ridiculous car. Fortunately for both of us, he chooses the brake pedal. Hey, I'm not trying to get ahead of him, I'm just trying to get out of this.

And my former lane buddy, still incensed at my lack of tact in occupying his spot in this river, salutes me with his horn as I swerve off the highway and onto surface streets. The sound of revving engines and honking misery Dopplers away behind me as I weave my way into a residential neighborhood.

I park re-Pete's little glorified golf cart of a car under a no-parking street sweeping sign, get out, thumb the lock on the key fob, then toss the key ring into a storm drain.

And then I start walking.

# 30

After a while of walking I emerge from an alley into a world of winners at the game of life, all hurrying to punch a clock so they can do some more winning. Some of them look at me with a face that screams "you don't belong here." Some of them are looking inwardly at themselves with that same face. I'm just looking for a phone number.

I find the light pole with my picture on it and tear a tab off just as I notice Cady up ahead, walking to work as she no doubt has hundreds of times on hundreds of identical days. She's carrying two cups of coffee in a cardboard carrier, a knock-off designer purse and the weight of the world on her shoulders.

I take out re-Pete's cell phone, punch in the number, and watch as Cady's pace slows and she reaches into her purse. She takes out a cell phone and I experience what has to be the happiest moment in my life as I realize I'm hearing her say "hello?" over the phone and not in the distance.

And then I experience what has to be the most painful moment in my life as I try to come up with a reply.

"Hello!" She comes to a standstill in a sea of foot traffic, a hundred homogeneous office drones with identical thoughts and feelings reshaping to flow around her like waves against a pier. It takes me a moment to figure out how to breathe again, and still, I have no idea what to say. "Hey, you know that homeless guy who's been stalking you? Well, I'm not, I mean, he's not such a bad guy..."

"I can hear you breathing," she says.

"I heard," I start to say. "You were looking for the guy. From the coffee shop. Why?" I feel like I just finished a marathon.

"Because I bought him a muffin and he owes me, that's why," she says. "Just kidding," she says with her free hand up like she's beckoning someone to come closer. "Hey. Do you know him? Are you him?"

I close the connection as I close the last couple meters between us, taking a position right next to her.

"Shit," she says, looking at her phone.

"Actually, my name is Kenny," I say when we finally make eye contact.

She throws her arms around me, almost dropping her phone in the process, then she peels back and throws a fist at my shoulder.

"That was so messed up!" she exclaims.

"Yeah, sorry, I was going to call but I'm not good with phones, then I saw you up ahead, and I thought maybe I should call anyway..."

"No, you big palooka, I mean the other day at the coffee shop, what the hell kind of weirdo saves someone's life and then confesses to a crime he didn't commit?"

"Oh. I'm." A palooka? "Sorry. About that guy," I stutter as passersby brush against us, annoyed at our failure to conform to the flow of foot traffic.

"Well, that makes two of us. But for different reasons." She grabs my hand and leads me to the edge of the sidewalk, out of the way of all the miserable pedestrians, then she pushes me off the curb to make up for the few inches of height difference between us. Now I'm standing in the gutter, she's standing on the sidewalk, and we're eye-to-eye.

"Listen, are you ok? I mean, things were a little tight for you, financially." she says before stumbling over her tongue. "I don't mean. I don't care. I mean, I do care, that's why I'm asking."

"I wanted to check on you, make sure you're OK," I say.

She hugs me again while saying "OK so we both care, glad we established that." Then she stands back and checks the time on her cell phone.

"Yeah, well I'm sure you're going to be late for work or something."

She gives me a look that cuts like a bulldozer. "Kenny, I could die a thousand deaths without ever living if work mattered that much. Or hey, better idea? I could just act like I'm dying." She coughs into her hand and starts wheezing like she just came down with the world's fastest case of pneumonia, then continues in a raspy voice. "I'll just tell my boss I'm sick." It's convincing.

She brightens up while pulling me up onto the curb with her, then continues in her regular, beautiful voice while looking up into my eyes.

"Will you wait here? I'll call you soon as I'm out." Without waiting for a response, she curtsies takes off down the sidewalk, the hem of her dress flapping against her legs as she skirts around the other commuters.

"OK," I think I manage to say. I'm not exactly Don Juan here. Don Juan with a concussion, maybe.

I stand like a statue observing the flow of traffic around me, and notice that no one seems to be arguing with anyone else. It's a moment of beauty; the passive aggressive body language and spiteful glares and all the normal negativity of a morning commute are utterly absent. Everyone seems to be united in some weird, cultish way, like they're all thinking the same thing. They're even looking in the same direction.

I turn to look in that direction and see re-Pete plowing past pedestrians, heading straight for me.

# 31

Elevator doors open into a plush office and out walks Cady with two cups of coffee in her hands, a bruised cheek and a smile that splits her face. She ignores coworkers who just stare at her resentfully while making her way past cubicles to the other side of the room.

She wipes the smile off her face, enters her boss' corner office and sets the coffee down on his desk.

"You're late," he says.

"I'm sorry," she says in her convincingly sick-sounding, raspy voice. He turns and looks at her as she starts spasmodically coughing all over the coffee.

"You're running out of sick days, you know."

"You think it might be contagious?" she asks, pointing at her nose. She sucks in some air through her nostrils so fast it almost collapses her nostrils, making her sound congested.

"Cady, you know what, I've been in the business of management for a long time. Can I give you some advice?"

Looking over his shoulder she sees re-Pete barreling down on Kenny in the street below and her face changes from sick to terrified. Her boss mistakenly interprets this as her reaction to his remark. He swivels his chair around to the window to take in the view while making his speech.

"If you want to be successful like me, you need to learn to hide your private life a little better. Do you think I get a corner office just because my dad owns the company? No, I showed up early, stayed late, and

I didn't let them see when I was sick. That's why I make the big bucks."

Through the window, he watches as Kenny turns, sees re-Pete, and takes off running.

"If I didn't have this work ethic who knows what kind of messes I'd be getting myself into," he continues, nodding toward the commotion outside. "Now if you ever want to make VP like me, you really need to figure out your priorities."

He turns back around and realizes he's been talking to an empty office.

There are benefits to being chased by people who want to throw you into a cold corner of hell, like the spontaneous exercise. And not being able to think about more than one thing at a time because of all the blood leaving your brain and rushing to your legs. And the spontaneous exercise.

I run as fast as I can along the same path I took a few days and a dozen lifetimes ago when I failed to escape from Santo. I even pass the same florist's shop, but skip knocking the display of potted plants in terra cotta vases into re-Pete's path. I've already crossed this one off my bucket list.

I make it around the corner, across the street, into an alley. Looking back over my shoulder, Re-Pete is actually gaining on me. If this weren't a matter of life or infinite death, I'd be impressed; I'm fueled by desperation while re-Pete is running on rage, and rage tends to win races.

A car screeches to a stop at the entrance of the alley. And I recognize that car. A familiar feeling washes over me as I find myself stuck between a rock and a re-Pete. Gotta try to clear that thing before Santo gets out and comes after me.

But instead of coming out, he leans across and opens the passenger door. "Get in!" he shouts.

It's weird how dying just a few times can make the interior of Santo's car suddenly look like everywhere I want to be. And there are worse things than going for a ride with this asshole; one such worse thing is going to get me in about three seconds.

I jump into the car and Santo peels away, slamming me back into the seat and almost slamming the door on my leg. There's a screeching sound of tires leaving their signature on the asphalt behind me.

As I lean forward to adjust my position in the seat, I get a glimpse in the side mirror of re-Pete still running.

And I lean back and almost miss her: Cady, running in the opposite direction, straight toward the very thing we're running away from.

# 33

She pushes her way past pedestrians to where she last saw Kenny, but all she finds are men ogling her in that disconcerting way men do when a woman looks distraught.

So she heads up the sidewalk along the same path Kenny took just moments before, hoping to get there before the cops do, determined not to let him confess to a crime he didn't commit just to escape his pursuers.

She passes a florist's shop and scores of well-dressed but douchey-looking office jocks. Some of them seem mildly amused, but most appear resentful that she's looking for someone other than them. She searches the face of every person she passes, hoping for a glimmer of attention not wholly devoted to her, but she comes up empty.

Suddenly, she hears tires screeching. She races around the corner in that direction, just in time to catch a glimpse of a black, two-door coupe as it accelerates past her. It's just a glimpse but it's enough to know the man who saved her life is in that car. With Kenny trying to haul himself into the passenger seat before the door closes on his leg.

She stops and redials the last number on her cell phone.

As the phone starts ringing, she looks up and sees the guy from the coffee shop. Not the one she held the door for, and not the one who killed her ex. The other one, the big creepy monster who appeared outside to direct the arrest, only to disappear moments later.

He meets her eyes as she puts the phone to her ear, and she feels that same mixture of fear and vertigo that she felt days ago outside the coffee shop. Except this time it's much more intense, like she stepped onto an elevator just as the cable snapped. Because before, he barely even noticed her.

Now, he appears to be very much interested in her.

And then the ringing on the phone suddenly stops.

"We have to go back and get her!" I shout.

"What do you mean we have to go back? I'm not going back!"

"But she's going to run right into him!"

"He's not a hurricane, Kenny, he's a gun, and that gun is not pointed at her!"

I crane my neck to see Cady as Santo takes us skidding around a turn, trying to gauge when and where to jump out of the car.

All of a sudden, panic takes over as something starts vibrating in my leg. I squirm around frantically trying to figure out what it is they've done to me. And then I really start freaking out when the vibrating is accompanied by what sounds like Mariah Carey crowing "Touch My Body" into a denim-covered Dixie Cup.

I pull the offending object out of my pocket; it's just re-Pete's phone. For a moment, all I can do is wonder what kind of monster has a Mariah Carey ringtone. But then I recognize the number on the screen. It's Cady!

But just on the fourth ring and right before I can find the little green button to accept the call, Santo snatches the phone out of my hand and slings it out the window.

"What the sweet hell was that?" I shout.

"That, my sweet hell, was a tracking device! Or did you think the guy who arrested you was a stripper going to a bachelorette party?"

I sit in sullen silence for a minute. I know he's right, but that doesn't make the reality he's cramming down my throat any easier to swallow.

"She'll be fine," he continues. "It's you I'm worried about, what the hell was up with that ringtone?"

"It's not mine, I took it off re-Pete."

"Re-Pete? Is that what you call the guy who was chasing you?"

I nod. "You don't know him?"

"I interviewed him, same way I interviewed you."

We pull up under a bridge, right under a no parking sign. Santo turns the engine off and looks at me before continuing. "And I rejected him. Because I didn't think I could handle him in one of those rooms, he was just too big. Probably why Prior thought he'd be perfect as my replacement."

"Wait a minute," I say. "What do you mean, you couldn't handle him? You mean like how you handled me?"

Santo closes his eyes for a moment, then nods. "I know how bad that sounds, and I know what I'm about to tell you is going to sound a lot worse, but Kenny? The last time you escaped? Wasn't the first time."

He lets a really painful moment pass before getting out, but I remain frozen in my seat, staring at his keys, wondering why I'm even tagging along with this asshole. I should be ripping his head off or running away, or both, and not necessarily in that order, but there's something I want to do even more than give in to my pain and rage. I want to escape it. And I want to take everyone with me, I want to save Ellie and Grazie and whoever else is in there, and I want to keep Prior from inflicting this nightmare on others.

A loud rapping on the window breaks me out of my train of thought. I look up to see him beckoning for me to follow, and with a real sense of urgency, so I open the door and step out. "Wait, your keys," I say, pointing back to the car.

But he's already hurrying across the street in an obvious rush, so I follow him to a heavily graffitied bench featuring a picture of a goateed, smiling lawyer in an ill-fitting suit. The ad next to the headshot says he's gotten his clients substantial sums of money in hundreds of wrongful death cases, and he can do the same for me.

A bus pulls up. Santo pays for both of us and we file to the back as the bus lumbers off out from under the bridge. Looking out the back window as we pull away, there's one of those pedestrian walkways on top of the bridge, the sort that's lined with bars and surrounded by rusty chain link fencing to keep people from jumping to their deaths. I can't help but wonder whether that's more to save lives or to keep the flow of traffic uninterrupted.

I turn to Santo. "So what happened the first time I escaped, did I reset you?"

"No, there was another guy who did and we just never opened the door for him after that. Took about a week for him to starve to death, but you? You never did more than you had to do to get past me and out that door. But once you were out, man, you were gone, I couldn't find you. Actually had to reset myself just to get you back in that room."

"And the second time?"

"I didn't even leave the building the second time." He mimics holding a gun to his head and pulls the trigger, making an exploding sound with his mouth. An elderly woman, overhearing this conversation, gets up and moves to the front of the bus.

"What about the third time?" I ask as the bus slows to a stop.

"I quit before the third time, and started looking for you pretty much immediately. Figured it might take you a month or more of trying and dying but it'd be like a day to me, and sure enough, that's when I found you. Let's get out here."

He hops out as the doors open and I follow. We head up a sidewalk to another one of those chain link and graffiti pedestrian bridges, which we use to cross over the highway.

"So what are we doing? Waiting till night then going back to get your car?"

"That wasn't my car."

"OK, then. What's the plan?"

He turns and looks at me. "Remember that thing you didn't want to talk about in the interview?" he asks, pointing at the tattoo on my arm.

I look past my arm like I don't know what he's pointing at and do the thing I always do whenever this topic comes up: I play dumb. "No, what would that be?"

The look on his face tells me how much I suck at playing dumb. "Kenny, in all the time I was there, you were the only one who managed to escape. So it's not like I got a long list of people to pick from, but you also have training that I don't have. And combat experience that they don't have."

"Santo. I was a medic."

"So?"

"So I trained to save lives, not throw them away. I'm literally the exact opposite of what you're looking for."

He looks at me for a second like he wants to believe me, but that look comes and goes, and then he just shrugs. "It's not like I got a long list of people to pick from," he says before he starts marching on again.

# 35

Cady tries dialing the number a couple times, but each time it goes to a generic voicemail greeting without so much as a single ring. She stares at her phone in frustration, not sure whether she should hit redial or 911.

Then she looks up and sees re-Pete staring at her, which gives her goosebumps. So she starts walking, trying her best to look like she doesn't have a care in the world, and she even manages to go a whole block before turning around to check, but he's still following her.

Maybe it's just a coincidence that he's walking in the same direction, she thinks to herself as she crosses the street in the middle of the slow flow of traffic. Some cars slow for her, a couple honk at her. One driver, mortally offended that someone would cross the street in front of him, peels out as soon as she passes his lane, almost sideswiping her with his mirror. But he spares her the injury while sparing himself the sort of insurance premium that goes with hitting a pedestrian, and she makes it safely across to the other side.

She goes another half a block of so before sneaking a glance, hoping against hope that he isn't still following her.

But he is.

"So, are we doing this?" Santo asks.

"OK, so let me ask, if we're doing this," I say as we ascend a sidewalk into suburbia. "What exactly is the this that we're doing?"

"We invade. Storm the building, take over the lab and figure out how to reverse the condition."

"Which condition?"

"What do you mean, which condition? Have you noticed what happens when you die?"

We enter the parking lot of the Shady Pastures convalescent home and hospice. I hope we're going inside to have a word with the owner about how creepy it is to have the word 'pastures' outside a facility where people take their loved ones to expire, but instead of marching up to the front entrance, Santo saunters past minivans and sedans toward the back of the facility.

"OK, so you know how to undo this."

We make our way around to a dumpster and a bunch of old cars, the part of the parking lot where long term residents leave their vehicles for days or weeks or months at a time to make room up front for visitors. "I'm an engineer. I put together pretty much everything in that lab," he says, stopping in front of a car so covered in sepia-toned dust and pollen that it looks like someone cropped it out of an old polaroid and photoshopped it onto the asphalt. He nudges a tire with his foot. In spite of everything else, it looks pretty sturdy.

"OK, so you know how to undo this?"

He takes out a knife with a little conical point on the pommel, the kind firefighters use to break windows, and grips it in his fist. "Not yet, but I understand the technology. It's like opening a car. If I have a key, I can move tumblers into precise locations such that I can turn the cylinder and get in. If I don't have a key, I have to find another way. Or make one," he says as he swings the butt of the knife into one of the rear windows, shattering it.

"It's about half understanding the technology and half trial and error. Just like with cars, spend a day sitting on broken glass and you learn to not break the window over the driver's seat." He reaches in through the rear window and unlocks the front driver's side door. "That's rule number one. Rule number two?" he continues as he gets down under the steering wheel. "Don't get caught. Actually, that should be rule number one." He feels around the edges of the console, finds the tabs and works the tip of the knife blade into them, popping just the first two, enough for him to get his fingers inside. Then he yanks down, hard, opening it up and exposing the barrel.

"OK, but what about the cancer?"

“What do you mean, what about the cancer? What cancer?” He pulls a wire out of a little hexagonal alloy box, rolls the end of it against the blade of his knife, then bends it against the blade. He holds it down with his thumb and yanks, stripping off a quarter inch of insulation.

“What do you mean, what cancer? That’s the condition we got from this condition!”

“Cancer? Huh. That’s a good one.” He strips two more wires then starts twisting two of them together in a smooth, practiced motion. “He was going to go with some kind of mental disorder, like we’re all going insane, because most people already wonder whether they’re going nuts anyway, right? But one of the people I interviewed had stage four cancer. Old lady, said she wanted to donate her organs but no one wanted them so she asked if she could donate her dying days to us instead. I bet that’s where he got the idea.”

“Wait a minute, are you saying I don’t have cancer?”

"I'm not saying you don't have cancer. I'm saying, if you do, you didn't get it from being a Reset. Why, are you disappointed?"

Of course I'm not disappointed, but I have to think about it for a moment because I'm not exactly relieved, either. I'm... I can't think of a word for what I'm feeling through all this anger. "Why would he lie about something like that?"

Santo pauses and looks at me. "Social Engineering 101. You want to own people, first you gotta convince them they're broken. Then tell them only you know how to fix them. Which is easier than you think, just act helpful. Human nature, we're hard-wired to trust people who act helpful."

"Did you learn that in engineering school?"

"No, Sunday school. And from the news. And politics, and beer commercials and love songs, but you want old school? Go to Sunday school." He touches the two twisted wires together against the third one, and the old engine growls to life. "There's a reason why bible colleges don't produce a lot of engineers but they do produce a lot of politicians," he says as he clips the console back into place.

He sits up in the driver's seat, leans across and unlocks the passenger door, then looks back at me.

"So, are we doing this?" Santo asks.

# 37

Cady winds her way around the street a couple times, hoping to lose the big guy following her, but even though he never looks directly her way he always seems to be going whichever way she's going. And he doesn't make even the slightest effort to look like he's doing anything else.

She's thinking about calling the cops when she sees a police cruiser coming down the street. She bolts toward it, ready to start waving her arms, hoping the officer will pull over. At this point, she'll do anything to feel safe again.

He pulls over! She waves at him while looking back at the guy who was following her. He's stopped, he's just standing there staring at her. Not so tough now, are you?

She looks back at the cop, ready to press charges, make a citizens' arrest, start a new war on terror, whatever it is people like her are supposed to do when they're afraid. But then the officer steps out of the car, and Cady does a double take. Even with the uniform and aviator shades and belt and gadgets, there's something about him that looks horrifyingly familiar.

# 38

I'm listening to the wind whistling through the broken window in Santo's stolen ride while wondering what I'm doing with my lives. And when and where might be a good time to jump out and run away. Not because I don't agree with the reason behind his plan, and not because the plan is stupid, but because we're up against a psychopathic genius with the power to put people in their own private hell, and I feel like maybe an insensitive engineer and a homeless medic aren't the right army for this kind of conflict.

And because every time I go to that building on my own free will, things don't seem to go so well. I know I'm basing this on a statistically insignificant sample size of realistically improbable experiences, but still. Experience tells me that going back by choice is a really dumb idea. And reason tells me that going back in a stolen car is even worse.

And especially right now, right this very second. I look around and recognize the road we're on and realize where he's taking us. My heart starts punching the inside of my ribcage.

"Relax," Santo says, noticing this. "We're just going to have a look around, figure some things out. No one's gonna see us."

He pulls into a suburban street a few blocks from the lab, parks under a tree and disconnects the two wires dangling under the steering wheel to kill the engine. We disembark and silently cut through someone's yard, following a bicycle path around the block and marching up a hill until we're on the crest overlooking the piece of recessed land in which Prior's building sits with those inch-thick sliding glass doors staring back at us.

The construction project around back looks idle; the foundation has been poured but the cement truck sits to one side looking lost and lonely, and there are no workers in sight. But there are a lot more cars in the lot than I'm used to seeing. Maybe they're inside getting a pep talk from Prior.

"What do you think?" Santo asks, handing me a small pair of binoculars.

"Are you asking for an opinion based on my military training?"

"Yeah."

I look through the glasses. "I think we could get two gurneys through those doors, side-by-side," I reply.

"I'm serious."

"So am I. That's the only door I've used, and I'm pretty sure the glass is bulletproof."

He shakes his head. "There's no such thing as bulletproof glass."

"OK, so what, we shoot our way in? Then what do we do when he calls the cops, shoot our way back out?"

"The last thing he wants is cops looking around inside that building. Anyway, it's the steel doors we have to worry about. Those are bulletproof, and the entrance is too narrow to drive a car through. Soon as they realize they're under attack, there's gonna be people behind those doors getting them closed. Lots of people," he says, pointing at the cars in the lot.

"New Resets?" I retrain the glasses on the entrance to the parking lot as re-Pete's big Town Car pulls in.

"Those are rentals. I'm guessing outside security."

I'm so shocked as I turn to look at Santo that I almost forget to put the binocs down. What's even more shocking is that he doesn't look as terrified as he should be; he either has a really good poker face or just doesn't know what his assessment means for his plan to storm the building below.

Normal security guards drive normal company cars, and there are probably a dozen such companies in this town alone. The ones who rent cars, on the other hand, do so because their sort of security service is highly specialized. The term we used for them in the military was 'civilian contractors.' We used that term because it didn't sound as morally abhorrent as 'mercenaries.'

"So it's you and me against a private army," I say as the Town Car pulls up in front of the sliding glass doors, just as it did when re-Pete last dragged me in there.

"That's one way to look at it."

"Well, then. I'm going to go look at something else for the rest of my lives," I say as I start to hand back the binoculars.

"Kenny," he starts to argue, but I'm not paying attention to him. What I'm suddenly paying attention to is re-Pete dragging another new victim out of the back of the limo.

I train the glasses on them again to get a better look as Santo drones on in the background about how he can't do this alone and he can't call the cops because cops will just turn the technology over to the government and the government cannot be trusted or something. It sounds like the sort of line an action hero would say in a movie and a conspiracy theorist would parrot on social media, but I can hardly hear him over the sense of dread that's swelling up in my throat and making my ears ring. It's like that feeling you get when you close your eyes during a scary movie to watch something worse in your imagination. Except my eyes are wide open and I'm not imagining this. She looks familiar.

I watch helplessly as re-Pete throws the struggling girl over his shoulder and she rains blows down on his back without him being even slightly affected. I'm trying to not let the memory of being in her position cloud my vision. It's not that I'm unsympathetic, I'm just trying to get a glimpse of her face while hoping against reason that it isn't who I think it is.

When he turns his back to me, I can finally make out who re-Pete is kidnapping.

It's Cady.

# 39

Everything is dark. I'm in a dream, swimming in a sea of grabby arms that are dragging me further from the light. I thrash and lash out at one set of arms in particular; they're attached to a familiar face belonging to someone bigger than me but not as big as re-Pete, someone I've managed to beat before in a fight. Or so he said.

"Kenny!"

I come to, still on the hillside, now with two hundred pounds of dirt and Santo all over me. It's hard to tell where the dirt ends and the Santo begins.

Even with my eyes wide open, all I can see is Cady being hoisted into hell on re-Pete's back.

I need to get Santo off me, and I know how to do it. I relax. And after a moment, he lets go his grip.

I immediately scramble back to the crest of the hill and look down again. Santo is on my back a fraction of an instant later, trying to keep me from running down there, but it would be too late anyway. The heavy glass doors are closed. They got her in there and I can't get her out.

I turn over, push Santo off me and sit up. He just sits there in the dirt, looking at me.

"You almost ran right down there," he says.

"You shouldn't have stopped me."

"So that's what it takes, huh?"

"Takes?"

"Nobody wants to save the world, most people won't even save themselves. But you see a pretty face and a skirt, and you're ready to risk everything. Lucky for me she's a looker, huh?"

"You make it sound like it's all just some base animal instinct." I get up and start walking down the hill, back to the car.

"Hey, whatever it takes, I'll take it," he says as he gets up and follows.

Re-Pete hauls Cady into the lab, drops her on one of the crossed-shaped tables like a sack of potatoes, and begins strapping her in. She resists with every shred of energy left in her, but she isn't used to fighting someone thrice her size, and her strength is waning.

Re-Pete goes about his work with his jaw set and his mouth clamped firmly shut. He acts like he's just carrying out any other ordinary, menial task, although from the look on his face, he hates the task almost as much as he hates himself for doing it.

Prior, sporting the same hint of a smile he had while killing rats, watches from his desk.

"Please, whatever I did, I'm sorry," Cady begs.

At this, Prior gets up, leaning heavily on his cane, and walks over to her. He brushes her cheek with the back of his trembling hand, then looks at re-Pete.

"Such a waste, wouldn't you agree, Peter?"

The corner of re-Pete's lip twitches as he struggles to keep his mouth shut.

"Rest assured young lady, you did nothing to deserve this," Prior continues, unmoved by the fact that he's the only one in the room who isn't profoundly unhappy.

"Then why am I here?" she asks through sobs and short, heaving breaths.

"That, my dear, is the question. Why is anyone here, hmm? Why did we come into this world, and why do we resist the inevitability of our departure?" He applies a small drop of glue to an electrode. "Philosophers and physicists and mythicists and many lesser minds have been pondering this point for millennia. Even as empirical reasoning techniques gave rise to new technologies and perspectives allowing us to look beyond our solar system and beneath our very skin, we continue to ask this silly question. Which is silly because the answer is as plain as this dot of glue on your brow," he says as he attaches the electrode to her temple with a flourish. "Our existence is its own reason. Or to put it a bit more succinctly, we exist to exist."

He adds another drop of glue to another electrode and continues, cutting Cady off before she can speak or even whimper. "One might even go so far as to suggest, as Descartes surmised, that our existence is proven by our capacity to reason. Which is quite ironic given that reason bestows upon us the capacity to observe the existence not only of ourselves but of others with barely the requisite intelligence necessary to put food in their mouths. No, reason is not a prerequisite to being, any more than intelligence is a prerequisite to success. Survival is the answer. We exist to survive and we survive to exist, until we cease to survive, after which point we no longer care."

"Are you going to kill me?" she asks, makeup-streaked tears running down her cheeks onto the table.

"Would it matter if you died by my hand or by the hand of another?" Prior asks. Cady looks at re-Pete and shudders. Prior smiles at this and continues. "I find it ironic that, inasmuch as you continue to be, you do so at the expense of other beings and yet you still have the audacity to question your place in the hierarchy of survival. Because your life, like every life in this wretched reality, depends upon the consumption and consummation of others. You exist to consume or to be consumed by another, and the question of which other is not yours to ask. If our paths had not crossed, you would no doubt fulfill your destiny in due time by the hand of some other fate, for fate has many hands."

He finishes attaching the electrodes, then moves back to his workstation and starts typing commands into the keyboard at the same desk where he killed his pet lab rat. "Actually, you are quite fortunate to have met me. Because, no, I am not going to kill you.

Instead, I am going to save you. Not from the death you fear, but from fear itself."

He finishes typing the string of commands, then hits the return key.

# 41

I sink into a chair in Santo's secret base and look around. We're in a trailer, and the dusty couch, kitschy-looking kitchen and the chintzy chair supporting my ass and all my misery tell me everything I need to know about his operational budget. The stolen car out front with the wires dangling under the dash looks right at home, at least.

We stopped on the way to swap out license plates with a Mercedes that was double parked in front of an all-you-can-eat buffet, and then we got gas and groceries while never saying a single word to each other. I've still got a lot of thinking to do, and Santo at least had the tact to give me some space and time in which to do it.

And what I'm thinking is we both want to get in there, but for different reasons. Santo's hell bent on taking over, while I'm just bent on taking someone out of hell.

By now, she's a Reset like me, or on her way to becoming one. She probably hasn't experienced her first, paralyzing death or the sense of insanity that follows through that next new day, because she's probably still too terrified to sleep. But exhaustion will take over soon enough, and then it will go from being the worst experience she could possibly imagine to unimaginably worse. And all because I went looking for her when what I should have been looking for was a bus station and a one-way ticket to elsewhere.

Santo sets a big heavy box down on the table and fixes me with a look that says we're on the same side. "There are two entrances to that building" he starts. "The main one in front and an emergency exit in the back. Except that backdoor was welded shut by yours truly. The idea being, if someone tries to escape, we block the front door and they run to the back. Then they're trapped in a corridor which we can close off like one of the rooms." He pauses for a moment like he's listening to himself, then continues. "I mean, they. Which they can close off like one of the rooms."

He shakes his head and hides a frown. "I was so proud of myself when I came up with all that."

He opens the top of the box but doesn't take anything out yet. "Anyway, that leaves us with the front door. The sliding glass doors are opened with an RF key card, but the steel doors behind them are manually operated. If someone tries to smash the glass doors, it should take a while, long enough for them to get the steel doors sealed. So the first step is smashing through the glass without taking a while."

He reaches into the box and starts removing the contents one-by-one, displaying them on the table in front of me. A Glock, a Beretta, a bunch of little cheapie Hi Point 9mms, a couple of revolvers... I lean my head sideways so I can look into the cylinder on one of the revolvers, and all I see is darkness. But it's not the vacant darkness of shadow, it's the heavy darkness of lead.

"Yeah, they're loaded," Santo confirms. "Takes less than thirty seconds to close those steel doors, and I don't know how many rounds it'll take to break through the glass, so any time spent reloading is time we can't afford to waste." He mimics shooting rapid-fire with a gun in each hand, then he mimics dropping the guns and grabbing two more. "We stand on either side of the door, put as many rounds into it as we can, and then eventually some of those rounds are going to go through. Followed by us."

"What happens to the rounds that don't penetrate the glass?" I ask.

"Doesn't matter. I bought cases of ammo."

"OK, general question here, what happens when a bullet doesn't penetrate a target?"

"It..." he starts to answer, but suddenly it hits him. "Yes! See?" he gestures excitedly. "That's the military know-how I need! OK, so we both stand on the same side of the doors."

And then it hits me too. I can't believe I didn't think of this before, Cady's in this mess because I woke up and went looking for her. So the solution doesn't lie in a half-cocked plan and a half-full box of guns. Call me an optimist, but one gun is all I need. And one bullet.

I grab the Glock, put the barrel in my mouth, and pull the trigger.

Click.

I realize the chamber's empty about a half a nanosecond before Santo's over the table and all over me, wrestling the gun out of my hand.

"I haven't gone to sleep yet!" I'm blubbering, I don't know if he can even understand me but I can't stop. "I woke up there this morning and if I can escape once I can escape again just let me do this all I have to do is not go looking for her!"

"You don't get it, do you?" Santo, Glock in hand, gets off me and starts packing up the box again. "You can't kill a Reset, all you can do is reset him. But then he comes back knowing how you killed him, so he has the upper hand, so then you have to send yourself back too, right? But what if he's just sitting there waiting for you when you wake up?"

“I’m not going to reset him, I’m just going to wake up and walk out!”

“It’s not that easy. You’ve only ever dealt with a shooter in a coffee shop, you haven’t gone up against a Reset before.”

“I went up against you.”

“Yeah, and you lost. On your own turf. You think you can handle Prior? He doesn’t even reset himself every day and he’d still see you coming.” Santo finishes packing up the box and moves it from the table to the kitchen counter behind him so he’s standing between me and the box. “How many times did you wake up in there, look around, and he wasn’t already in his lab? Or walking the halls? Or waiting around a corner somewhere? I worked there, hell, I ran that place, and I never once woke up before Prior. That’s why I went looking for you. That’s why I need a partner, to keep him alive while I work, because if I mess up and kill him? He wakes up and has the upper hand. If I lock him in one of those rooms? He’ll kill himself and he’ll still have the upper hand. Any way I go about this alone, I give him the upper hand, and you do not give the upper hand to a psychopathic genius!"

"OK, I get it."

"No, you do not get it," he says, weary with rage. "You feel it, and that's not the same thing. That's not even close."

"I messed up," I start to say.

"What is it with her, anyway? Why's she so special?"

"You wouldn't understand," I finish. Somewhere between those two statements is a whole thesis on how I got into this mess because I trusted the wrong person and then I dragged someone else into this mess because she trusted me, but I can't figure out how to say it without pointing out that Santo was the link before me in this whole chain reaction of misplaced trust. And I don't want to piss him off, because I'm weak and exhausted and can't hope to beat him in a fair fight, and I really need one of those guns.

But he picks up the box and starts walking into the bedroom on the other end of the trailer, saying over his shoulder as he goes: “We’ll talk about this in the morning. Or not.”

He sets the box of guns down inside the bedroom, then turns back to look at me. “You can crash out on the couch if you want. Lock the door behind you if you don’t.”

He shuts the door.

A moment later, I hear the lock click into place.

Cady, in a state of shock and bewilderment, is escorted down the hallway to hell by re-Pete. They stop outside one of the doors, which he unlocks and opens.

She peers into the darkness, then looks back at re-Pete, her eyes brimming over with fear and hate. He meets her eyes with the same look, but his is directed inward. She asks, "what did you do to me in there? I thought you were going to kill me."

Now he can't meet her eyes anymore.

Suddenly, she bolts. But he gets an arm around her waist and hoists her up, kicking and punching as hard as she can. Which isn't very hard; she has barely a fraction of the energy she had when he carried her into the building. But now it seems to be affecting him.

He starts to carry her into the room, but she manages to get one foot up on either side of the door jam.

Instead of pushing through, he steps away from the door, turns around, and walks backward with her into the room where he turns around again and gently sets her down. Then he quickly runs out of the room, shutting the door behind him.

She throws herself against the door, then melts to the floor, too weak to stand. There's a bit of light coming through the crack at the bottom of the door, broken in the middle by the shadow of re-Pete standing outside.

The shadow stays there for a good long while.

Then it leaves.

"Hello?" she calls after it.

# 43

I lock the door behind me just like Santo asked. Not because he asked, and not out of habit, but to give myself an extra second or two in case I need it. And it's not like I'm coming back.

Quietly, I open the door to the stolen car and sit myself down in the driver's seat. I don't even know what kind of car this is, I never pay attention to these sorts of things. But I did pay attention to how Santo started the engine. Twist two of the wires together and touch them against the third. They're just dangling there, a couple inches apart. Makes me wonder, if the windows were open and if a strong wind were to pick up, whether this thing could start itself.

I twist the first two together and get ready to touch them to the third wire, but first I look behind me at the short gravel driveway and the dark road beyond it. It's clear; no lights in sight and nothing blocking my way, so I turn my attention back to the wires in my hand and touch them together.

The engine roars to life. Quickly, I put it into reverse and start backing down the driveway, stopping just short of where the gravel meets the pavement. Looking back at the trailer, the lights remain off and the door doesn't open. Guess I didn't need that extra second or two after all.

I back out onto the street and take off.

Dying is kind of like skydiving. It doesn't get boring after the first few hundred times, though you do want to start looking for new ways to do it. Which is why I want to go looking for a cliff to drive off of. But I've lived in this town long enough to know it'll take more than a tank of gas to get me to the nearest ledge suitable for suicide, so I head out to find a freeway instead. A good, solid concrete divider will do, as long as I have enough space to build up some serious speed.

Seriously, Santo's insane if he thinks his plan is better than mine. All I want to do is rescue an innocent person, while he's basically going to storm a building full of professional soldiers, and he thinks he can pull it off with a bitter medic, a bit of moxie, and a box full of hand-me-down handguns?

I can travel back in time to before the mercenaries arrive and accomplish my task without anyone even seeing me. All I have to do is die, wake up, and get lost. And I'm good at all those things. Especially getting lost.

Hell, I'm lost right now. Somewhere in my train of thought I missed the freeway and found myself driving aimlessly. I look around and recognize the road I'm on and where it leads, and realize I'm just a few blocks from the Prior Institute. Which makes me wonder; most people, when they go on autopilot at the end of a long day, wind up driving themselves home. Because home is where the heart is, unless you're homeless.

Well, Prior was already up and working when I rolled out of bed this morning, but he didn't seem to be aware of where I was in the building until I moseyed into his lab and told him I was leaving. And I can't get what Santo said about never giving Prior the upper hand out of my head. What if he's better prepared this time? Getting out of the building is only half the battle, getting away from it could become more complicated. It wouldn't hurt to scout the area and find another route out of there. Just in case.

I pull up into the same residential neighborhood where Santo and I parked earlier today, disconnect the two twisted wires under the dash, and get out, following the bike path and marching up the hill in an almost total absence of light. The sky above isn't so gloomy because I happen to be on the dark side of the world right now, it's just overcast. And ugly. Thunder crashes in the distance, and I can tell a storm is coming, but it doesn't matter. In about twenty minutes from now and twenty hours ago, I'm going to walk out of that building under a clear sky. And then I'll be long gone, long before they can figure out which way I went.

Because Santo mentioned an emergency exit on the other side of the building that'd been welded shut. So what I'm thinking is, when I walk out the front, I'm going to circle around the back to the last place where they'd think to look for an escapee and take off from there in a new and completely different direction. If I can, that is; if it's fenced in or full of brambles or anything else that will slow me down, it would help to know that in advance.

I start picking my way down the side of the hill toward the building with heavy glass doors and the pitch black emptiness behind them, when I notice what appears to be the light of a firefly flickering down by my ankle. But when I glance down, it's gone.

Then it reappears after a couple more meters, and since I'm not seeing more of the little critters around me, I stop to look. And what I see isn't a firefly. It's a little yellow dot. I move my ankle back and it disappears. Move my ankle forward again and it reappears.

I'm stepping through the motion sensing beams of a perimeter defense system.

All of a sudden, the building comes to life as lights both inside and out come on. A loud beeping alarm, loud enough to penetrate the walls and reach me at this distance, goes off from deep within the building. And men in combat gear start to assemble behind the heavy glass doors.

The lights come on in the room and Cady's eyes fly open.

The sound of a key turning in the lock is so loud it makes her wince. She sits up and moves to a corner.

The door opens and re-Pete steps inside. "What do you want from me?" she asks, hugging her knees, too weak to defend herself from rape or whatever worse thing he has in mind.

He just looks at the floor for a moment. Then he reaches into his pocket and takes out a long, thin object, which he holds out to her.

She shakes her head. He looks back down at the floor again.

"I'm sorry," he says. "I..."

Suddenly, a loud, beeping alarm goes off, so loud it manages to startle re-Pete. Cady clamps her hands over her ears.

Re-Pete drops the object in the center of the room and runs back out, slamming the door shut behind him.

As the alarm continues to scream from somewhere deep within the building, Cady moves out of her corner into the center of the room to see what it is that re-Pete dropped.

It's a protein bar.

# 45

I race back up and over the hill, not waiting to see the doors open or count what's coming after me. Because I know what I'm going to be up against, and while I don't know how much of it there is, it wouldn't matter if I did. My entire knowledge of fighting boils down to the stun and run, basically baiting someone into a sucker punch and then sprinting. But these aren't the kind of guys you can stun, and they aren't the kind of guys you can outrun, either.

But running is my only option at the moment, so running is what I do, back down the bike path, through someone's yard and around the side of a house to the street. I see the car parked up ahead of me, but I know I won't make it in time to figure out which wire is which, get the engine started, get it in reverse, and get out of range.

I'm ready to start yelling and waking up the neighbors just as huge, fat droplets of rain start hitting the street, turning the blacktop blacker and drowning out all other sounds. A bolt of lightning tears through the sky above followed immediately by a loud crack of thunder, bathing everything in light and sound for half a second. Then everything goes back to wet darkness. No one's going to hear me in this torrent, and even if someone did, they wouldn't run out to help. The only thing running in this mess is water down the storm drains.

One such storm drain sits under the curb right where I came out of the neighbor's yard. I dig my fingers into the manhole cover but it's heavy and rusted, no way I'm going to move this without a crowbar. So I flatten myself onto the asphalt in front of it and start to shimmy in sideways, but then I just wind up sandwiched between the rough iron lip of the storm drain and a patch of pavement not worn smooth by tires running over it. I reach down inside and manage to leverage myself the rest of the way, barely making it through and shredding my shirt in the process. And then I fall about four feet to the bottom.

I pick myself up out of the filth and litter just as a pair of black tactical boots hits the street in front of the storm drain, followed by another, and another, and then three more in rapid succession. Six pairs of boots attached to six sets of black slacks, black shirts and black bag operators fan out over the street. I can tell they're professionals because they aren't just looking for movement; they're looking for any sort of hiding space and anything else that's out of place, peering behind, under, and in cars, and taking particular interest in the broken window and shiny new plates on my stolen ride.

Another pair of feet lands on the pavement in front of me, this one sporting the sort of sensible sneakers favored by conversationally challenged bodybuilders. Re-Pete comes into full view as he steps away from the gutter to join a pair of mercenaries in front of my car. They confer about something, leaning in while raising their voices to be heard over the storm, but their voices don't make it across the street and through the rain to my ears. All I can do is wait and watch as re-Pete takes out a phone and calls someone. And as the water starts to rise around me.

The other guys start heading back, stepping over my storm drain one-by-one. They came up wet and empty but don't look the least bit bothered about it, unlike re-Pete, who looks like he wants to pick up and throw the car down the street. And he looks like he could.

I examine my immediate surroundings, what little there is. There's a big, wide pipe at about my hip level that the water and sticks and litter is draining off into. That pipe might be my only way out of here. It's wide enough to fit me, though I don't know how long it'll stay that way. And it isn't completely submerged in water and filth yet, although again, I don't know how long it'll stay that way.

A flash of red and blue light yanks my attention back to the street. A cop car pulls up next to re-Pete and my stolen ride. The window opens just a crack, enough for re-Pete and the cop to talk, not enough to get the cop wet. I can't see him from here, but I have a feeling I'd recognize him if I could.

They finish their conversation and re-Pete starts walking down the street, probably taking the long way so he won't muddy up his soggy shoes. The cop car backs up and pulls in behind my stolen ride, his engine running but the lights off. By now, he's run the plates and realized they belong to a shiny new Mercedes and not an old whatever the hell that thing is. Which means he's just waiting for the tow truck to arrive. Which means I won't be crashing into a concrete divider tonight.

I look at the pipe that's filling up with water and debris and start to feel claustrophobic. If I drown in there, I'll wake up in a warm bed in the building on the other side of the hill. If I make it out, I'll still have to find a bridge to jump off of. If I stay here, I'll get too cold to climb back out, and it's not like I have a car to climb out to. Or enough shirt left to protect me.

Oh, what I wouldn't give for a cliff to drive off of right now. Or a bridge to jump off of, or some oncoming traffic to run into. It's not that I'm afraid of death, I'm just terrified of drowning. But what's waiting for me out there is worse.

I take a deep breath and crawl into the pipe.

# 46

Cady comes to on the cold tile floor and takes in her surroundings. The light is on; she looks up at the ceiling tiles around the bare bulb above her and wonders for the umpteenth time whether she could get out through them. Then she looks at the walls, even though she already knows she won't be able to climb them. Then she looks at her fingernails, marveling that they're intact.

She sits up and confirms that her body is unventilated and there's no blood on the floor, just the untouched protein bar by the drain in the center of the room. Nothing she hasn't already seen or considered; this room wasn't exactly designed to engage or entertain, at least not the occupant.

But then she notices something she hasn't seen before: a spider, just inside the door. "Hello," she says, and then pauses politely, long enough to allow him to reply but not so long as to make it awkward. "I'm Cady," she continues. "And you're Boris. Boris the Spider. You don't mind, do you?" She puts her weight on her hands and brings her knees up under her. Boris skitters to the side an inch or three in anticipation of her next move. "It's OK," she says with her palms up before bringing them back in close to her body; a reassuring gesture to humans might look like an attack to an arachnid. "I'm not going to hurt you."

The door opens and a big foot in a wet but sensible sneaker enters, stepping on Boris and squooshing him into the tile floor. The rest of re-Pete follows the foot just in time to see Cady kneeling there with her mouth open, staring at his shoe, clearly upset.

"Sorry," he says as he unfolds and sets down a metal chair just inside the door. He stops when he sees the uneaten protein bar on the floor and moves to snatch it up, but he freezes like a deer in headlights when she finally meets his gaze. Her eyes, full of shock just a moment ago, are empty and unfathomably deep now. He's seen that look before and should be getting used to it by now, but actually the opposite is happening.

Prior walks in behind him and stops, leaning heavily on his cane, to stare at the protein bar for one long, lingering moment. Then he raises his eyes to re-Pete, who looks like he just stepped back from a precipice. Re-Pete does his best to put an apologetic look on his face, even though he knows no amount of acting skill will save him.

Prior takes a semiautomatic pistol out of the pocket of his lab coat, his eyes still on re-Pete. "Peter? What did I say about feeding them?"

"What did you say? You said don't feed them."

"That is right, Peter. I am sure she looks small and manageable." Prior moves the slide back on the pistol just a quarter inch, enough to verify that there's a round in the chamber. Satisfied, he lets the slide snick back into place. "But looks can be deceiving."

He takes a seat, crosses his legs, and smiles like he's about to enjoy a nice cup of tea. Then he finally gazes into Cady's eyes, and unlike re-Pete, he doesn't experience the least bit of vertigo.

"Cady, is it?" he asks, pointing at her casually with the gun. "I must apologize, as I believe we got off on the wrong foot. Would you mind terribly if we were to start over? I am Doctor Ethan Prior, founder of the Prior Institute, which you might think is a remarkably prescient name once you come to understand the nature of our research. Or perhaps you already do?"

"One," she replies, deadpan.

Prior snaps his fingers at re-Pete, who holds the tablet in front of Prior at eye level. Prior presses the big go button at the bottom of the screen with his other hand, the one not holding the gun, and watches as numbers scroll down the screen, stopping eventually on the number one.

Satisfied, he looks back to Cady. "So we have had this conversation before. Now I cannot help but wonder. Why are we having it again?"

# 47

I come to in a darkness so dark I have to blink to know my eyes are open. I'm on a cold, wet concrete ledge of some sort, and for a few seconds all I know is how much I dislike cold wetness and concrete. I don't remember where I am or how I got here.

Then it all comes flooding back to me. The tunnel I'd climbed into and spent what felt like hours inching through was just one of many leading into this larger chamber, which is a pretty ironic place to get stuck. Ironic because, if my sense of direction is correct, this places me more or less right under Prior's parking lot. And stuck because there's a steel grate blocking the tunnel that leads out of here. And there's about a bazillion tons of trash trapped in the grate.

Water was still flowing through, but not fast enough to keep the room from filling up. At first, I tried grabbing handfuls of branches and trash and throwing them behind me, but they just flowed back around me to clog the thing up again. So I started feeling around under the water and filth for something sturdy enough to lever open my exit, and I did manage to find a piece of rebar attached to a clod of concrete and gravel. I started swinging the piece of rebar against the wall to break off the chunk of concrete. By the time I finished that, the chamber had filled up to the point where my feet weren't on the floor.

Now this is just one of those things you don't think about until you're treading water in a concrete cage full of garbage, but maybe looking for a more exciting way to die wasn't one of the best choices I've made in my life.

But I didn't think about it for long, because I have a deep aversion to drowning. I attacked the steel grate with the piece of rebar, eventually ripping a bolt out of the concrete and leveraging up a corner. Then I got a foot in sideways and start bending it back with my leg until the water and trash started flowing through again. I'd been doing all of this in the dark, rising up to a concrete ledge to take breaths and then pushing myself back under the filth to work on the grate. I was running out of air and couldn't afford to take a break, so when I finally got it open enough to get through, I went back to the concrete ledge to rest for a moment. I reminded myself over and over again, as I lay there feeling colder and wetter and more exhausted than I ever remember feeling, to not close my eyes.

Then I woke up. The good news is, if I get killed today, I'll wake up in a place where no one will find me. The bad news is, that place is here. And the worse news is, I won't just wake up and waltz out of town like I'd planned.

I sit up on the ledge and hit my head on the ceiling a few feet above me. Then I lean sideways and let myself fall back into the water, which isn't nearly as deep as it was before. Whether this is from my work or the rain stopping, I can't tell. I can't even guess what time it is or how long I've been down here.

I feel my way back to the steel grate and peer through into the tunnel beyond. There's a little bit of light in the distance, not much, but enough to give me hope and get me moving. I climb into this tunnel like I did the last one and the one before that and start crawling toward the light.

Eventually I am delivered through a corrugated metal opening into a muddy creek, covered in goop and grime and just as ugly as the newborn day. Everything is more or less the same color; the water around me is just a shittier shade than the overcast sky above and what's left of my shredded shirt. I wade through clay and crayfish to a muddy bank, and from there up past trees and debris into a middle-class suburban neighborhood where I almost run face-first into the most terrifying thing I've ever encountered.

It's a man. A normal, clean man wearing a department store business casual outfit while holding a stainless steel mug of coffee in one hand and a muffin in the other. He looks like the embodiment of every life goal I've ever failed to realize. I bet he smells terrific.

He stares at me for a moment, in my soggy shirt accessorized with dirt and sadness, and it occurs to me that he should be as afraid of me as I am of him. But he's not. Instead of running or calling the cops, he smiles and holds his breakfast out to me. "Here," he says. "Get some calories in you. The storm isn't over."

I want to say something in return, but I don't know what words are or how to use them. So I just stand there trying to look nonchalant while holding his breakfast. He climbs into his sedan, backs out into the street, and drives off to join the rest of the world.

# 48

The gravel on Santo's driveway crunches under my wet feet as I trudge the last few steps to his little aluminum door. I raise a hand to knock, but it opens before my knuckles touch it.

He doesn't interrogate me, doesn't bother to ask how my mission went, can't even muster an 'I told you so.' He just turns around and walks back to the kitchen table like I'm late for breakfast.

I set my ass down and sit my new coffee cup on the table next to a collage of chaos: piles of pistols and stacks of ammo boxes cover more than half of the Formica surface, each gun a messenger, every bullet a message. Santo doesn't make any move to keep them away from me. He finishes loading a clip, puts it next to the corresponding weapon, then starts loading another one. I wait and watch in silence until he finally opens his mouth.

"You look like shit," he says. I nod while he finishes another clip and starts a new one. He looks like he has something more to say, but he just sits there looking like that while thumbing bullets into clips one-by-one. So I lean in and reach for a magazine and some ammo, figure I'll get to work.

"Nah, here," he says, pushing a different box of bullets my way. "Use a hollow point if you're gonna reset yourself."

"I'm not going to reset myself."

"Fine, then." He goes back to loading the magazine in his hand, the spring becoming tighter and harder to manage with each additional piece of devastation. As an engineer he probably understands these weapons better than I do, but I can tell from his clumsy pace and lack of rhythm that he hasn't handled them much.

I take a box and a clip and start loading. "I've been wondering," I start to say.

"Getting her out of hell isn't going to get hell out of her," he says, cutting me off. "You can't save her, you know."

"How'd you do it?"

"Do what?"

"Work for him. For Prior."

He fumbles one of the rounds; it skids off the table onto the floor. He pushes his seat back to reach for it, but pauses and just stares at it on the grimy old carpet. "It's hard to explain. I got hired as an engineer but then found out I was going to be sort of an orderly, too, like in a psych ward. Which wasn't what I signed up for, but engineers get all kinds of weird work, and I figured a job's a job, I'll keep the inmates inside, keep them safe. That's what I told myself. I didn't know where this job was going to go." He picks the bullet up and carefully presses it into the clip with his thumb. "But next thing I know, it's like I'm one of the inmates too. By the time I figured out what was going on, I was in way over my head. I still can't explain it."

"I helped overthrow a sovereign government on the pretense of non-existent WMDs," I say. "You don't have to explain it to me."

"But that was just the beginning, see. That new construction project on the side of the building? There's bodies buried in that foundation. I know because I laid that foundation. Had to buy a cement mixer for it, because when you rent a cement truck it comes with a driver, and you know, drivers get weird when you ask them to pour concrete over a hole full of faces. But it didn't start out that way. I got a job, signed a non-disclosure agreement, filled out a W-4, and then I died. Which sucked, but you know what sucks more than dying? More dying. So I stuck around looking for a way out while digging myself deeper into a moral hell on top of the infinite hell of never-ending death which, by the way, I'm probably going to be spending on death row now. Because bodies don't stay buried. So yeah, that's how I did it."

I look at the table in front of me; I'd been loading magazines while he talked, and my stack is now as big as his. "I screwed up," I say.

He shakes his head and picks up the clip he hasn't yet finished loading. "What happened, she dump you?"

"It wasn't about that."

"Of course. It wasn't about your heart, it was about your hard on. You wanted to put your junk in her trunk."

"It wasn't about that either."

"OK, then what was it?" He sets the clip down and sits back, arms crossed, waiting for my story.

And so I finally tell it.

"I was on a wait list at the VA for therapy, which felt like being on a waiting list for the lottery. It was the best and only option I had, I couldn't hold down a job, I couldn't even sleep at night. I was working construction, trying to make rent, just trying to make it to the next day. One day, the last day, I get a text telling me the job's been cancelled. I'm in line at this coffee shop trying to count out change in one hand while checking a text with my other, and I have enough coins for coffee or a muffin but not both, and whichever one I get, it's going to be my last one for a while because I'm out a paycheck. And I'm avoiding looking at this girl in line in front of me because she's nice, I see her there every day, but this isn't the worst day of my life, it's like icing on a cake made out of all the worst days combined, and the girl's looking at me funny and I just can't do small talk. So I stare at the text on my phone until I get to the front of the line, and the guy behind the counter, he gives me a coffee and a muffin. I tell him no, just the muffin this time, and he points at the girl who's on her way out the door. And she turns around and says 'that's your usual, right?'"

I reach for another clip but we're all out of empties. So I just stare at all the hardware on the table. "Right then and there. I decided I wasn't going to wait for a bed to open up at the VA, I was going to get better no matter what it took."

"You went through all that because someone bought you a muffin? That's what changed you?"

"Isn't that what changes anyone?"

"I don't know, I'm more of a donut guy myself."

I don't want to laugh, but I can't help myself. "You know, you're pretty funny when you're not murdering me."

"Thanks for noticing."

"Thanks for not murdering me."

He points at my shiny new coffee mug on the table. "She buy you that too?"

"No. This was just some guy who saw me and decided I needed it more than him."

"Now you gotta save him too? Is that why you're here?"

"No. I'm here because I woke up in the middle of a burning forest, and I went from trying to save myself to trying to save my favorite tree to finally seeing the rest of the ecosystem and realizing that what I really need to do is attack the flames before they spread. Prior's going to sell that technology, isn't he?"

"Eventually. He's trying to extend his own life first, so he shifted from testing and proving the tech to developing it further, but yeah. He's definitely gonna sell it."

"Is that why he started recruiting again?"

"He never stopped."

"So there's going to be a lot more Resets."

He nods.

I stand. "When are we doing this?"

He sizes me up for a moment, then sighs and stands up with me. "Right after we run a couple errands. And get something to eat. Can't save the world on an empty stomach."

"I'm sorry I lost your car," I say as I follow him to the door.

"That's all right. You can steal me a new one."

# 49

"Where are we headed?" I ask. We've been walking under this overcast sky for a while now, not much by my standards, but all the walking adds up.

"You'll see," is all he says in reply. Like I can't guess; we're headed up the side of a four-lane road that veers to the left and ends in the parking lot of the kind of store you go to when you need pants and pizza and a kitchen sink in a hurry. Dressing up to shop there is like pairing wine with hot dogs, it's just not something people do. Which is good news for what's left of my ego; I won't be the only one in there looking like I got crapped out of a drain tunnel.

Sure enough, as we turn the corner and the store comes into view Santo holds his arms out in a sweeping gesture and presents my destiny. "Ta-da! Your one-stop shop for tools, toiletries and t-shirts. I'm thinking we oughta get you something with a corporate logo on it. So everyone will know you didn't just pay for the product, you also paid to advertise it."

"You're killing me, Santo."

"Why do you have to keep bringing that up? I said I'm sorry."

And so we go the rest of the way bantering like characters in a cancelled sitcom till we reach the store, where everyone glances first at me with sympathy or disgust and then at Santo like he's some sort of saint. He looks like he's taking a homeless man shopping, and he relishes it like a comedian basking in a laugh break. Underneath the magnanimous façade, I can tell he isn't used to being seen as the good guy.

We go inside to the food counter and spend the next few minutes eating reconstituted meat products with tomato syrup on denatured bread. It's not quite as good as some of the dumpster fare I've enjoyed in recent weeks, but it's warm and it beats MREs.

Then we finish our meal of protein and preservatives and hit the clothing aisle where I pick out a new pair of shoes, pants, and a t-shirt advertising a movie I've never heard of. Santo even springs for a new belt. And then we head toward the home improvement section where we pick up a pack of extra-long zip ties. I explain what they're for and Santo just shakes his head. "Once a medic, always a medic," is all he says.

We're about to check out when something catches my eye: a whole rack of crowbars, big, beautiful, black-painted pieces of iron and leverage. I veer off in that direction with Santo in tow and pick one off the rack, hefting it in my hand.

"We need this," I say.

"What for?"

"You'll see."

"Where're we headed?" he asks. I'm fueled up and breaking in my fancy new outfit, feeling like someone set back my odometer by about a hundred lifetimes. I don't answer him because I don't care where we're headed, I could walk all day feeling like this.

We turn a corner onto a residential street with posted signs warning people to move their cars once a week for a street sweeper that never comes, and right under one of those signs, nestled in the gutter with the rest of the trash, sits re-Pete's little glorified golf cart of a car. It's sporting a coexist bumper sticker like a tramp stamp on the back, which I somehow hadn't noticed before, and it's covered with a fresh new layer of dust interrupted by a fresh new parking ticket.

I wad up the parking ticket and toss it into the storm drain. Then I wave my hands over the car like a game show model. "Ta-da!"

"You're kidding."

"Too small?" I ask, hefting the crowbar.

"Too alarmed. Don't steal a car where you have to steal a key first, Kenny. Pick an old one. With manual locks. And a back seat."

I walk over to the storm drain, get the blade of the crowbar under the manhole cover, and lever the thing open. Takes a bit of work but I'm able to get the lid off and set to the side without making too much noise or throwing my back out.

I let myself into the drain feet-first as Santo rambles on above me. "And a decent engine. And a sense of self-respect. You can't enter these things from the bottom, Kenny. Kenny? OK, that's it, you lose your turn. I'm stealing the next one!"

I fish around in the muck and murk at the bottom. If there's any one thing I've learned from hanging out in storm drains, it's that they're not very efficient at moving trash. And sure enough, after a moment, I find what I'm looking for: a key fob. I press a button and am rewarded with a satisfying beep of a car alarm disengaging.

I pull myself out of the storm drain, still relatively clean and none the worse for wear, so I can bask in the glow of Santo's approval. Or better yet, his disdain. Or whatever the hell that look on his face is supposed to represent.

"Do I even want to know who you stole this from?" he asks as we get into the car.

I turn the engine over and strap myself in. "I don't steal, I borrow. In this case, from the guy who stole your old job."

"Oh yeah? When were you planning on returning it?"

I look up through the windshield at the overcast sky. The storm is coming back.

"Seat belt."

# 51

Cady comes to on the cold tile floor and takes in her surroundings. The light is on, the walls are solid, and her nails are intact. There's a protein bar on the unbloodied floor, and by the door sits her only other friend in this entire world, a tiny spider.

She rolls to her side and addresses him. "Boris?" She sits up and continues without waiting for a response, knowing he won't mind. "Let me ask you something, if we've had this conversation before, why are we having it again? I mean, not to interrogate you,

I'm really curious. Do you remember any of this before? Like, do you know what's going to happen when that door opens?"

She puts her weight on her hands and brings her knees up under her. Boris skitters to the side an inch or three, enough to show he's alive but not enough to remain that way. "You shouldn't be here," she says. "Don't take this the wrong way, it's not that I don't appreciate your company, but if you don't get out, you're going to get into a fight with a foot, and you're going to lose."

As if on cue, the door opens and a big foot in a comfortable athletic shoe enters, stepping on Boris and squooshing him into the tile floor. The rest of re-Pete follows to find Cady kneeling there, staring at the floor with a grim look on her face. He pauses for a moment, a folding metal chair in one hand and a tablet in the other, then he notices the uneaten protein bar on the floor by the drain. He tries to open and set the chair down quickly so he can snatch the snack, but between being rushed and not wanting to drop the tablet in his other hand, he drops the chair.

It clatters to the ground just as Prior walks in behind him and stops, leaning heavily on his cane, to stare at the chair and the protein bar for one long, lingering moment. Then he raises his eyes to re-Pete, who looks like he just got caught with his hand in the cookie jar.

Prior takes a semiautomatic pistol out of the pocket of his lab coat, his eyes still on re-Pete. "Peter? What did I say about feeding them?"

"What did you say? You said don't feed them."

"That is right, Peter. I am sure she looks small and manageable." Prior moves the slide back on the pistol just a quarter inch, enough to verify that there's a round in the chamber. Satisfied, he lets the slide snick back into place. "But looks can be deceiving."

He takes a seat, crosses his legs, and smiles like he's about to enjoy a nice cup of tea. Then he finally raises his eyes to meet Cady's, but stops when he sees the index finger on her right hand raised like a bidder at an auction.

"Excuse me?" he asks, gesturing casually with the gun.

She points at the tablet in re-Pete's hand. Prior's eyes follow; he snaps his fingers and re-Pete comes over quickly to hold the tablet in front of Prior at eye level. Prior presses the big go button at the bottom with his other hand, the one not holding the gun, and watches as numbers scroll down the screen, stopping eventually on the number one.

Curious, he looks back to Cady. "So we have had this conversation before. I cannot help but wonder. Why are we having it again?"

Her lip starts quivering. "I keep telling you, I don't know." She sits back against the wall and braces herself for the bullet.

# 52

"The trick is getting through the glass doors before they can close the steel doors behind them," Santo says. We stopped along the way at Santo's secret base to pick up his box of guns, and to kill some time. Now we're lying prone on top of the same hillside where we originally scouted the building about a bazillion years ago, looking down into a parking lot littered with cheap rental cars and weird memories from lifetimes ago. "We gotta approach real quiet, they can't know we're coming until the first shots are fired."

"Quiet isn't going to work," I say, pointing at the ground about two meters in front of us. "There're motion sensors all over the side of the hill, which means there are probably motion sensors all over the property."

"Huh. How do you defeat motion sensors?"

"Two ways I can think of. One's slow, one's fast."

"I like fast," he says with a grin.

We inch backward till we're far enough out of sight to stand, then walk back down the bike path to the car. I hit the button on the key fob to deactivate the alarm and we climb inside the cramped vehicle just as the first few fat raindrops hit the windshield. In the seat behind us are two fifty-pound backpacks. Santo turns and pulls one up to the front, setting it on my lap. I unzip it and look inside to make sure all the guns and magazines are neatly ordered while Santo pulls the other backpack forward and does the same.

Then we set the packs on the floor between our feet and lean the seats back.

Santo fiddles with his wristwatch. "What's a good time?"

"Ellie, the old woman, she said she wakes up at three and she's the first one in the building to rise."

"Three it is," he says as he finishes setting the alarm. "We're probably gonna die, but that's OK. The first run is recon, see what we learn. Make sure you get some sleep so we can reset here."

I nod and close my eyes. The rain is really starting to pick up. I'm exhausted and sleep should come easy, but being anxious to get started works, being anxious to get to sleep, not so much. I start going through a mental checklist of all the tension in my body, relaxing the muscles in my face, neck, shoulders, and back, but I'm having trouble dozing off.

So is Santo. After a few minutes of fidgeting failure, he turns to me. "It really bugged you when I shot that guy in the coffee shop, didn't it?"

It's a weird memory to go back to, so much has changed between then and now. But the way I feel about killing people hasn't. "Yeah. It really did."

"He wasn't exactly a peach, you know."

"Was that your first time?" I ask.

"First time killing someone?"

"Who wasn't a Reset."

"Yeah," he says after a moment. "But it was him or you. I mean, I get it, he couldn't come back so it wasn't really him or you. Lemme ask you something, how many times did he reset you?"

"Six."

"Because you were trying to keep him alive, right? How many times you think it would have taken if you'd just gone in there and finished him?"

"No way to know. In there, maybe twice. In the space between my ears? I would have spent the rest of my life reliving it."

"Well, I hope saving the world is enough to offset what you're about to do in the space between your ears. Because if we succeed at this, some people might die. Normal people, not Resets. At least you'd better hope they're not Resets."

"Just aim low, OK? And don't you die on me."

"If I die, I'm taking you with me."

"Do you have any idea how creepy that sounds?"

The sound of him trying to suppress a laugh answers my question.

I close my eyes again, and this time, I'm out like a light.

# 53

BAM! My eyes slam open to the sound of Santo's wristwatch going off. He fumbles around in the dark for a couple seconds till he finds the button that cancels it.

We breath for a moment to adjust, then we get out and stand under the moldy sky, cold rain falling around us like dead stars. It's a surreal and familiar feeling, like that that feeling I'd get before combat when I realized I might die. Except this time, I'm not the guy in the back of the truck with a bag full of medical supplies. And this time, I don't just think I could die, I'll be surprised if I don't.

I strap on my bag full of murder supplies and start marching with Santo by my side. Not a word is spoken between us as we work our way around the houses, up the bicycle path and to the top of the hill overlooking Prior's building.

We turn our backpacks so the straps cross our chests and the bags hang at our sides, under our arms. Then we each take out two guns, one in each hand. Then we look at each other and nod.

Then we start running down the side of the hill, sprinting through the rain and wet grass as fireflies light up around our ankles. We make it about halfway down before the building below lights up, an alarm sounding inside.

We take up our positions on one side of the door with Santo standing under just under the eave and me a few feet further out in the rain. There's movement inside, soldiers manning the steel doors. We raise our guns and start firing in the cold rain, bullets slamming into and ricocheting off the heavy glass doors. It takes just a couple seconds to empty the first four guns, but cracks are already starting to form on the glass.

We drop the first set of guns and reach into our bags taking out two more each, and we start to fire, but my shots go wide. One of the raindrops hitting my shoulder felt hotter and heavier than an ordinary raindrop, throwing off my aim and pushing me down. A couple more hot and heavy raindrops follow, and I realize what's hitting me isn't water. I look up as I fall to the asphalt and see men on the roof with rifles.

It occurs to me that I can't tell the difference between the rain and my blood pooling on the dark asphalt. Then the pain hits me and I do that thing I've seen so many men do on the battlefield before me: I start screaming.

I'm on my back, trying to turn sideways so I can better see what's going on, but bullets are hitting the ground around me and I can't keep my eyes open as little pieces of lead and asphalt pepper my face and neck. The shooters on the roof aren't killing me, they're trying to use me as bait to draw Santo out from under the roof. Or maybe they aren't killing me because they know what I am. I try reaching into my bag for another gun, but my arm doesn't work. Neither of my arms work. The only thing in my body that seems to be working right now is my central nervous system, but all it's doing is howling at me. And all I can do is howl back.

I look up just in time to find myself staring down the barrel of Santo's gun.

BAM! My eyes slam open to the sound of Santo's wristwatch going off. He fumbles around in the dark for a second till he finds the button that cancels it.

"Not so creepy now, huh?" he asks.

I blink my eyes and shake my head to clear the pain that's no longer there. Technically it never was, but I'm still too woozy to contemplate the paradox. "Did we get the door at least?" I ask.

"Almost. Couple more clips would have done it I think."

“We’re going to have to stand closer.”

“Promise I won’t fart.”

Somehow, somewhere along this journey, I went from dreading every uncertain moment of my waking life to this unexpected feeling of... purpose? Is that what this is? Takes me a moment to realize it, but I’m actually looking forward to whatever happens next. Who’d have thunk that dying could be so much fun?

“Remember to save your last shot,” Santo continues. “In case we need a mulligan.”

“You’re hilarious.”

We get out of the car and adjust our packs as we march up the bike path to the hill again, not stopping at the top but rather sprinting straight down through the wet grass and motion sensors. An alarm goes off and the building lights up as before. We start unloading the first two guns on the doors before we finish crossing the parking lot, taking up our positions side-by-side in front of the glass doors and right under the roof.

We unload a pair, drop them, get out two more and keep going, aiming for the same point on the glass doors. A crack starts to form as the mercenaries start closing the steel doors behind it. And the crack is growing, but not fast enough. I drop a pair of guns and start to reach for two more, knowing I won't get them out in time as Santo lunges with his boot at the door. The first kick bounces off and he almost loses his balance, but he regains his footing and the crack doubles in size with the second kick. I prep a pair of pistols, ready to cover him just as his third kick drives through, shattering the glass into a million glittering pieces.

But the steel doors click into place, and I realize we're too late just as a bullet slams into them. Santo looks at me in alarm; both of my guns are down and his hands are empty. We've been flanked.

We jump to positions just inside the doorway, in the space between the steel doors and where the glass doors used to be, each to one side. I'm guessing the shooters on the roof came down the side of the building and took up positions behind cars in the parking lot, but the air in that little space is too leaden for me to lean and assess.

And then I look down and realize I'm bleeding; I hadn't noticed through all the adrenaline, but the bullets hitting the steel wall are turning into white-hot shrapnel and shredding my skin as they burrow down and bury themselves in muscle.

And now that I see this, the pain hits me. Hard.

"Your turn!" Santo shouts over the din.

"But you haven't been shot yet!"

"You can have the honor!"

"Rock paper scissors!" I shout back through the metal flying between us.

We hold our hands up close to our sides and out of the way of gunfire, and pump our fists in unison. One, two, three. I come up with a rock.

He comes up with a middle finger.

I raise my gun and blow Santo's brains out all over the wall behind him, just before a bullet from the parking lot plows through my hand and shatters my wrist.

The gun goes clattering to the ground. I reach into the bag under my arm with my remaining hand and pull out another one, hoping it already has a round chambered since I don't think I can work the slide one-handed.

I put it to my temple and pull the trigger.

# 55

BAM! My eyes slam open to the sound of Santo's wristwatch going off. He quickly finds the button that cancels it.

"You need to learn the rules," I say.

"Winners write their own rules."

"Then start writing faster, will you?"

"I'm working on it."

"Could we lever the doors open with a crowbar?"

He shakes his head. "The motor that holds them shut is too strong. Only thing a crowbar would be good for is shorting out the electrical system underneath it, but the access point is on the other side of the doors."

"OK. So what's our next step?"

"I said I'm working on it."

So am I. The glass isn't bulletproof, it just takes a lot of bullets, and that in turn takes a lot of time. So the key lies in shaving off those critical few seconds we lost to the motion sensors.

But then I look at the key in the ignition and remember I don't have to steal the key to steal the car. I just need to find another way to light that spark.

"Where's that crowbar?" I ask.

"I told you, you won't get enough leverage."

"I'm not going to use it for leverage," I say as I lift my butt out of the seat and take my belt off. "Remember when you said the entrance was too narrow to drive a car through?" He looks at the tiny box around us and catches on quickly. The entrance is only too narrow for an average-size car; but this thing's way smaller than average.

I loop my belt around the steering wheel then turn the engine over and put the shifter in drive. It takes a bit of trial and error with the belt and a couple zip ties, but I figure out how to jury rig it so that the steering wheel won't turn. Once I'm confident it'll work, I cut the zip ties with Santo's knife and prep a couple more. Then Santo hands me the crowbar, which I place on my lap.

We pull out of our parking spot and head down the street. A couple turns takes us to the entrance of Prior's parking lot.

I floor the gas pedal and drive straight in, the building lighting up as motion sensors alert them to our presence. We skid to a stop outside the heavy glass doors and Santo gets out and runs behind one of the cars while I back re-Pete's car up to give it as much distance as possible.

I'm still getting the car into position when the first round comes through the windshield, tearing through the passenger seat. I can hear the pop-pop of Santo returning fire, and I look up to see the shooters on the roof taking cover. I can also see mercenaries behind the glass doors getting the steel doors into place. With just a little more turning, I get the car so it's pointed directly at the entrance, then I set the brake, put it in drive, and rig the belt and zip ties to lock the wheel into place. And then I wedge the crowbar between the seat and the gas pedal.

I get out as the tires start spinning on the wet asphalt. Santo's still trading shots with the rooftop as I lean back into the car, one hand on the dash, the other on the emergency brake. I release it with one hand and quickly push off the dash with the other, barely getting my head clear of the cabin as the tires stop spinning and find purchase. The car takes off.

I get two guns out and start running after it with Santo close by. And then I witness the most awesome thing I've ever seen: the car gains momentum as it hits the ramp in front, then it launches a couple feet up into the air and smashes through the heavy glass doors.

But then it smashes into the steel doors a fraction of a second later, airbags going off and the front end crumpling against the impenetrable barrier. There's enough of a dent now to know that the steel doors as about as car-proof as the glass doors were bulletproof. Which isn't helpful because I'm shit out of cars.

A bullet slams into my hip, knocking my ass back and making me lose my balance. I instinctively let go of the guns in my hands so I can catch my fall. As I hit the ground, another bullet tears into my back and through my guts before ricocheting off the pavement and tearing back up through even more of my insides. I can see Santo out of the corner of my eye falling too, as my blood goes septic and my vision gathers into a tunnel. I try to reach for one of my guns but all I see and feel is a bottomless black void.

# 56

Cady comes to on the cold tile floor and sits up with a start. "Boris," she says to the tiny spider by the door. "Don't take this personally, and don't ask me how I know, but you gotta get out of here." She puts her weight on her hands and brings her knees up under her, then slowly stands, forcing herself to move despite hunger and exhaustion and the memory of all the injuries that haven't happened to her yet.

She makes it all the way to a standing position before all the blood rushes out of her head. For a moment, the room becomes brighter and she forgets who she is and how she got here. Then it all comes rushing back to her as the head rush subsides. She pushes the memory out of her mind and lurches forward, hoping to shoo Boris back out through the crack under the door, but he runs up the wall instead.

"Well... yeah, that's probably good enough," she says, wheezing from the effort.

Just then, the door opens and Cady stumbles backward, stepping on and smooshing the protein bar on the floor as re-Pete enters with a folding chair in one hand and a tablet in the other. At first, he's surprised to see her up on her feet, but surprise turns to sadness when he sees his stepped-on gift by the drain. And then that look quickly turns into fear as he stumbles over himself trying to pick it up.

Prior walks in behind him and stops, leaning heavily on his cane, to stare at the protein bar for one long, lingering moment. Then he raises his eyes to re-Pete and is about to say something when he sees movement out of the corner of his eye. He swings his arm and smacks it against the wall, crushing poor Boris' carapace into the unyielding surface. Then

Prior looks at the mess on the palm of his hand and holds it out to re-Pete.

Re-Pete untucks the corner of his shirt and dutifully cleans the dead spider off the palm of Prior's hand with it. The old man inspects his hand, and satisfied, takes a semiautomatic pistol out of the pocket of his lab coat, his eyes still on re-Pete. "We are going to have a little talk later, aren't we, Peter?"

"Are we? Yes."

Prior moves the slide back on the pistol just a quarter inch, enough to verify that there's a round in the chamber. Satisfied, he lets the slide snick back into place. He takes a seat, crosses his legs, and forces a smile onto his face. Then he finally meets Cady's eyes.

"Cady, is it?" he asks, pointing at her casually with the gun.

"One," she replies, deadpan.

"Excuse me?"

She points at the tablet in re-Pete's hand, and re-Pete holds it up at the seated man's eye level. Prior jabs the big go button at the bottom of the screen, the one not holding the gun, and watches as numbers scroll down the screen, stopping eventually on the number one.

He looks back to Cady. "So, we have had this conversation before. I cannot help but wonder why we are having it again."

"I keep telling you, but you just don't understand." She slumps back against the wall and braces herself for what she knows is coming.

# 57

BAM! My eyes slam open to the sound of Santo's wristwatch going off. He cancels it.

"Was that you or them?" I ask.

"Bit of both," he says through clenched teeth.

"Thanks."

"Don't mention it. Seriously." He's holding still, just breathing, but I can tell he's running a sort of mental checklist on his body to verify it isn't riddled with holes.

Death is never easy and he hasn't learned how to deal with the shock of a particularly brutal one yet. I'm not going to offer advice because that would just be rubbing in the fact that I've had a lot more experience than him, which in turn would rub in the fact that he's the one who gave me most of that experience. Instead, I think of something to say to help get his mind off the pain and back on the plan. "Would have worked if we had a few more cars, huh?"

"Or a few more parking lots."

"Or bigger guns. Or body armor. Or," I'm just spitting out whatever I can think of to keep him talking, but an idea starts to form in my mind. "Or more rain."

He looks at me like I'm the one in shock now. "More rain?"

"I was thinking about what you said, about shorting out the electrical system under the door. What if the rain were to flood the door and shut it off for us?"

"Yeah that'd be nice, except there's a whole drainage system under that building and the surrounding streets. We're going to need a lot more than just a lot more rain."

"Maybe we just need a lot less drainage." I look around in the tiny little hatchback trunk space behind us, find the crowbar, rest it on my lap the way Santo did a lifetime or so ago. "You ready to get wet?"

We leave the guns in the car and lever the lid off the storm drain, then carefully lower ourselves into my old hiding place. Santo bitches the whole way, but me, I can't wipe the grin off my face. I shouldn't get such a perverse pleasure out of putting him through this, but there's no one I'd rather have in here with me.

Once we're inside, I look up and see a few threads snagged on the lip of the inlet. They're the same color as my last t-shirt, and I silently promise myself I'm going to carry a crowbar with me everywhere I go for the rest of this life. And the rest of the next one, too.

I squat in front of the tunnel and prepare to lead the way. "Please tell me I'm not going to die in there," Santo says.

"Relax. You're probably not going to die in there. If you do, we'll just meet up back at the car, right?"

"Yeah, if you die too. We shouldn't have left the guns."

If he's worried about another difficult death, I can't blame him. But his tone of voice tells me this fear runs deeper than drowning. "wait, what do you mean?"

"Kenny, if one of us resets, we both have to reset."

"You mean..." I stop to think it through. Every time I died alone, I went back and watched the world play out like someone'd hit the rewind button. But every time I reset with Santo by my side, we died together and went back together. It hadn't occurred to me before, but... "What happens if one of us dies and the other doesn't?"

"I don't know."

"What do you mean, you don't know? Didn't you guys do tests on this?"

"Tons! But it's not something you can observe directly unless you're testing on yourself. You walk into a room thinking you're gonna perform an experiment on someone, right, but that someone's a Reset, so first you have to ask whether you've already performed the experiment, but the guy you're asking is in too much shock to talk, or too terrified to string two words together, or, what happens most of the time, actually, he's trying to kill you. After a while they're all trying to kill you, which makes it really hard to interview them. So you think, what if I put two of them in a room together and reset just one of them, what happens then? What happens is you're in a two-on-one fight. Every time you go in there to kill one of them, you wind up fighting both of them, so you never wind up performing the experiment."

"OK so what, if you die and I don't, where does that leave me?"

"I don't know, Kenny, that's the point! We're talking about time travel, and we don't even understand what time is! That's why I said if I die, I'm taking you with me."

"Well, that went back to being creepy again real fast."

“Says the guy who hangs out in drain tunnels.”

Says the guy who killed the guy who hangs out in drain tunnels, I want to reply. But we’re not getting anywhere by talking, and he’s getting defensive now, or maybe that’s me.

I turn back to the tunnel and start inching my way in.

# 58

Crawling through drainage systems is really low on my list of fun things to do, even lower than finding new and exciting ways to die. But while crawling through storm tunnels is low on the list, waking up in one is even lower.

And it's not the sort of thing I'll ever talk about in polite company. I'm picturing myself at a party, a glass of cabernet in one hand, listening as someone tells me what an ordeal medical school was before I counter with an observation about with how hard it was to crawl through a pipe under a building in which I'd been killed a hundred times with my only friend by my side, who happens to be the very same guy who'd killed me a hundred times in the building above us. Yeah, if I ever have a social life again...

"What's so funny?" Santo asks behind me.

"Nothing," I shout back at him over my shoulder, realizing I'd been laughing out loud. I go back to my daydream, in which the guy I'm talking to is the yuppie I met the last time I crawled out of this tunnel. We're chummy and impeccably dressed in this fantasy, and in one hand, I'm holding a glass of wine, while in the other, I'm holding Cady's hand.

OK, I can admit this to myself now, my feelings for her are about more than an act of kindness. I just hope she's all right. I've been pushing her out of my mind because there's nothing I can do for her except keep inching forward while hoping against hope that it's not too late to save her.

"What's the hold up?" Santo asks behind me.

"Nothing," I shout back over my shoulder, realizing I'd stopped moving.

I drag my mind back into the moment and keep putting one hand in front of the other until we arrive at the large chamber under Prior's building. It's still full of sticks and filth and the metal grate is still bent back from the last time I came through, but everything looks smaller now. And more crowded.

"So what's your plan?" Santo asks.

"This is the last stretch of tunnel." I pull on the metal grate and let it go with a wet thwanging sound, then dip into the water around us and pull up an armful of sticks and litter. "This grate was clogged last time I was in here, almost to the point where I was running out of air. I had to move a ton of trash and bend this thing inward to get out." I start sticking branches and bits of trash into the grate. "So we bend it back into place, clog it up again. I think all the runoff from all the surrounding streets flows through here, and it's right under the building, so we stop the flow and let it fill up and flood the parking lot."

Santo pulls back on the metal grate and lets it go with a thwanging sound. Then he looks around the room like he's measuring it. "I'm sorry," he says.

"What?"

"What I said back there, calling you the sort of guy who hangs out in drain tunnels. I belittled your reason for being here, which means I belittled you, and for that, I apologize."

"Oh." I want to say he's forgiven, but what comes out instead is "sticks and stones may break my bones, but I'm a Reset so you're going to need something more substantial."

"Good, because I don't want you to take this the wrong way, but sticks and stones aren't going to be enough. Water's still going to get through, and even if you do manage to stop it up completely the buildup will create an ebb and flow that'll just break it up again. You're gonna need something more concrete." He pulls back on the grate again and peers into the pipe past it. "Like concrete. But more than we can carry."

"OK. Well, scratch that plan," I say.

"Where does this go?"

"Past the houses down the hill. It lets out into a creek."

"Could you get a truck into that creek?"

"Yeah. If you don't mind getting your truck dirty."

He puts a boot on the grate, bending it back further. "Don't scratch that plan yet," he says as he climbs into the tunnel.

# 59

Cady comes to on the cold tile floor, rolls onto her side, and looks at Boris. "I tried," she says. "I don't think you know how many times, I don't think you'd be here if you did. Or maybe you would? I'm only just starting to figure this out myself."

She sits up and continues. "All that worrying, yeah, it was for you, but it wasn't about you. It was about me. That's my thing, I worry. And that's not my only thing, I've got anger and fear and… I've got other things. I used to blame them on others because who else, right? But I understand something now. You're going to die and there's not a thing I can do to stop that and I'm not at all happy about it but I can still accept it and appreciate you and not go cold and hard and lose feeling over it. And I wonder if you can too. I wish I had more time to find out, but you're about to die again. And so am I. And here's the thing, here's what I figured out: fear doesn't change anything. Fear is pointless. So I'm not afraid anymore. Bye, Boris."

The door opens and a big foot in a comfortable athletic shoe enters, stepping on Boris and squooshing him into the tile floor. The rest of re-Pete follows the foot just in time to see Cady sitting there with a sad smile on her face. He's seen a lot of looks in these rooms but he hasn't seen that one yet.

"Sorry," he says as he unfolds and sets down a metal chair just inside the door. He stops when he sees the uneaten protein bar on the floor and moves to snatch it up, but between Cady's sad smile and his hands being full, he's too confused and clumsy. The chair clatters to the floor.

Prior walks in behind him and stops, leaning heavily on his cane, to stare at the protein bar for one long, lingering moment. Then he raises his eyes to re-Pete, who can do nothing more than look back at him with the same mixture of fear and guilt and shame and loathing that Cady's seen on his face now more times than she can remember. It dawns on her suddenly that she feels the same concern and worry about him that she felt about Boris, despite everything she's been through. And she feels it for Prior as well, despite everything she's about to go through.

Prior takes a semiautomatic pistol out of the pocket of his lab coat, his eyes still on re-Pete. "Peter? What did I say about feeding them?"

"What did you say? You said don't feed them."

"That is right, Peter. I am sure she looks small and manageable." Prior moves the slide back on the pistol just a quarter inch, enough to verify that there's a round in the chamber. Satisfied, he lets the slide snick back into place. "But looks can be deceiving."

He takes a seat, crosses his legs, and smiles like he's about to enjoy a nice cup of tea. But then he finally gazes into Cady's eyes, and for the first time, he recoils. What's staring back at him is disconcerting, something he's never seen before.

"Cady, is it?" he asks, pointing at her with a firm grip on the gun. "I must apologize, as I believe we got off on the wrong foot. Let us start over, shall we? I am Doctor Ethan Prior, founder of the Prior Institute, which you might think is a remarkably prescient name once you come to understand the nature of our research. Or perhaps you already do?"

He waits a moment for her to reply, long enough to be polite but not so long as to make it awkward. But Cady's unblinking regard still makes it so.

He snaps his fingers at re-Pete, who holds the tablet in front of Prior at eye level, and presses the big go button. Numbers scroll down the screen, stopping eventually on the number one.

Prior looks back to Cady. "There is a number on this screen. Can you tell me what it is?" It occurs to him, when she doesn't reply, that perhaps she's injured or mentally impaired. Or maybe she's just ignoring him. Not a gambit that's been tried before, but not entirely implausible. "Can you speak?" he asks. Another uncomfortable silence passes. "Perhaps you can show me with your hand the number on this screen."

She slowly raises her hand, breathes in, then exhales while raising a single finger. The middle one.

It occurs to him that, between the kindness in her eyes and the defiance on her finger, she might be mad. Which is quite rude on her part, as he is giving her every conceivable chance to conform like a normal human being. He grips the pistol even more tightly and takes aim.

"Our mutual friend, Kenny. I would very much like to speak with him again, if you should happen to know his whereabouts." He waits just a moment, not so much to let her reply as for emphasis, then he shoots her in the leg. She arches her back and throws her arms out, grabbing onto the floor like she's trying to keep from falling through it, but she doesn't cry out or even gasp. A single spent shell casing hits the floor with a dull, melodic tone that no one can hear over the ringing in their ears.

"I've rather taken a liking to that boy, as I imagine you have," Prior says loudly while slowly aiming the gun over other parts of her body. "Which I imagine due to a certain lack of harmony between your actions and your failure to answer this simple question. You see, when we found you, you were looking for him and he was looking for you, which would seem wholly unremarkable if not for the fact that people tend not to look for those whom they do not know. And so, since you must indeed know him, I should assume you might also be able to help me locate him."

He continues pointing the gun at different parts of her body like a painter hovering over a canvas, looking for the perfect spot to lay down a stroke of red. Cady takes a deep breath and closes her eyes.

He shoots her in the other leg. She bites back a sob while holding onto the floor.

"I conducted a little experiment recently," he continues in a raised voice while she quietly bleeds out. "We know that torture does not yield useful information. Prevailing wisdom suggests this is due to the subject's willingness to say anything necessary to end the pain. Personally however, I think this owes to the fact that one can only inflict so much damage before ending the subject, because all the king's horses and all the king's men could not put a dead person together again."

He finds another target on her body and puts a bullet through it. "We are going to need a new set of nursery rhymes. Kenny Mulligan. The man you were seeking, who was also a subject in this very same experiment, we learned quite a lot from him. We learned that people tend to surrender once they begin to grasp the inevitability of death, only to begin their fight anew once they begin to grasp the infinite nature thereof. Although it does appear to take quite a lot of dying before one arrives at this understanding. Our friend Kenny died hundreds of times in the course of this experiment, but you, dear Cady, you can be spared that knowledge by answering one simple question."

"You're asking the wrong question," Cady gasps with what little life and breath she has left.

Prior lowers the gun. "And what, pray tell, might be the right one?"

She tries to smile around the rictus of pain, but what bleeds through instead is a strange and beautiful sadness. “Who are you really hurting?”

“Fascinating. I have seen so many forms of defiance in these rooms, but smug morality is a new one.” Prior raises the gun and shoots her again. “How long do you think it will it last? We lose our fear of certain things when we become accustomed to them, and death just happens to be one of those things, but I wonder. Will you ever become so accustomed to pain?”

He takes aim and fires, then takes aim and fires again.

# 60

At least I get the easy job, I think to myself as I settle into position. I'm at the top of the hill overlooking Prior's facility with a gun in each hand and my bag of death beside me. At any moment, that building might light up. If that happens, some well-armed and highly-trained guards are going to come running out, and my job is to shoot at them. With pistols. From this distance. So basically, I'm here to stress out a bunch of mercenaries. At least I get the easy job.

Santo looks like an ant from up here as he slowly approaches the construction site. His job is to steal the cement truck, if he can do so without tripping the alarm. If he can't, his job will be to scout out the rest of the motion sensor system, which is why I'm here: to buy time.

He walks slowly in a straight line, scanning side-to-side for protruding pieces of plastic. Personally, if I were down there I'd just run right up to the truck and see what happens. I expect I'd die anyway so once more wouldn't be a big deal. But Santo's really hoping to pull this off on the first attempt.

I pull the slide back on one gun just a half an inch or so, enough to see a dull brass shell casing resting in the pipe. I do the same with the next gun, then I unzip the bag next to me. Any moment now, I'm going to rain hell down on that construction site. I'm actually supposed to fire at the guards to slow them down until my own position is overrun, but I'm not going to waste a lot of ammunition on that. I've seen guys like them work before, and I know better than to hope I'll be able to buy Santo more than a minute or so. And buying him time isn't as important to me as making sure he dies, because I just don't know what I'll do if they take him alive.

I point one gun at the building and the other at my friend, waiting for the lights and alarm, ready to unleash lead. Santo carefully puts one foot in front of the other over and over again until he reaches the truck. Then he opens the cabin, leans inside and starts fiddling with the dash.

A light comes on in the building; it's go time. There's no alarm yet, but professional people poachers are going to come pouring out those doors any second now. I hear the sound of a diesel engine coming to life in the distance; Santo got the truck started, at least. He hauls his butt up into the seat, closes the cabin door and slowly starts backing out of the construction area. I look back down at the building, ready to start shooting, but still no one's coming out.

Then I look to the sky and see that one side is slightly lighter than the other. It's not quite dawn, but the light in the building was probably just someone waking up and getting breakfast. I wait until Santo is clear of the construction site, then I wait a few more minutes to be sure they aren't just letting him go so they can follow him.

After a while, I pack up my bag and start walking back to the car, as shocked as I am elated that it worked out. This bodes well. I hope.

# 61

There aren't a lot of places you can park a cement truck without standing out, but one such place sells cement. And coffee, and clothes, and kitchen sinks, which makes it a great place to gather supplies and for killing time. Which is good for us since we're about two inches of rain and twelve hours away from killing anything else.

We park at the ass-end of the monster lot and walk into the store, Santo still sporting that magnanimous grin, at least for the first minute or so. But he's as scruffy as I am now, and people aren't looking at him with the same smiling approval he got before. In fact they aren't even looking at him at all, just passing with the same sort of peripheral awareness normally afforded to things like structural support beams and the homeless. I can see he finds this disconcerting; even sale signs and the candy aisle get more attention. If aliens were to base their entire assessment of the human race on this place, they'd think we worshipped sugar and discounts.

We eat, then I stop by the bakery to pick up a pack of muffins before heading over to the hardware section where we load up a cart with bags of quick set concrete mix and one long PVC pipe with a screw-on cap. Then we bring the truck around to the back. I lift the bags one-by-one in front of the drum, Santo cuts them open, and we dump the contents inside. A sales associate lets us borrow a hose which we use to pump water into the drum. Then we turn it on and take off with Santo leading the way while I follow close behind in re-Pete's little toy car.

We're armed to the teeth while going just under the speed limit. Because by now, either of the vehicles we're in have probably been reported as stolen, which means that, if one of us gets pulled over, we're both going to have to commit reset by cop.

But we find the access road to the creek and manage to make it there without killing ourselves or anyone else. I crawl into the tunnel, jury-rig the metal grate to slow the flow, then we build an improvised structure of sticks and zip ties to hold the cement at the entrance of the tunnel. The PVC pipe goes at the bottom of our makeshift rebar contraption to let water through so it won't build up and wash out the concrete before it sets. Then we back the truck up to the tunnel, lower the chute, and push and squish and shovel cement in with our hands until it's sealed. In a couple hours we'll come back to screw the cap onto the PVC pipe.

"I'm gonna ditch the truck under an overpass," Santo says. "Follow me?"

"Which overpass?"

"About a mile up the street. Last one we passed on the way here."

"I'll meet you there," I say, shouldering my bag of metal and mayhem. I climb the muddy bank and walk past trees and debris into a middle-class suburban neighborhood.

I can hear the diesel engine of the cement truck starting up behind me as I round a corner to what I've come to think of as the Muffin Man's house. His car is in the driveway but he's nowhere to be seen. It's later in the day, which means he probably has the day off, which is just as well; gratuitous displays of gratitude make me uncomfortable.

I reach into my bag of guns and ammo, take out the stainless steel coffee mug, and place it on the hood of his car. Then I take out the pack of muffins and place them beside it.

Then I walk back to re-Pete's piece of crap car, get in, and head off to the overpass to meet Santo.

Re-Pete sits at his desk in the lab, next to the crucifixion tables, mechanically typing away at his keyboard. It's data entry, the most boring task imaginable, but not the entirety of his job. Unfortunately.

His eyes wander to the gun on Prior's desk.

He shakes his head and turns his dead eyes back to the work in front of him, entering a number, doublechecking it, entering another, again and again. Then his eyes wander back to the gun. Try as he might, he just can't stop looking at it.

That girl in the room, what she went through, what they all went through and are still going through and will continue to go through... that could have been him. He's supposed to be the lucky one. But he doesn't want to live with luck like this.

Finally he gets up, looks around the room, and seeing no one, picks up the pistol, points it at his temple, squints his eyes as tightly closed as he can get them, and smiles with relief as he lets out one last breath. Then he pulls the trigger.

Click!

His eyes fly open in alarm, he racks the slide back and looks at the nothingness inside. The chamber's empty and so is the magazine below it.

"What time did you wake up this morning, Peter?"

Re-Pete spins around to see Prior standing behind him, leaning on his cane. "What time did I wake up? Five," re-Pete replies.

"Perhaps I should apologize," Prior says as he steps forward, his hand extended, palm up. "It isn't appropriate to taunt someone of your disposition with such a question, what time you awoke matters not a whit. That you refrain from wasting my time, on the other hand, is of the utmost importance. Are we clear?"

Re-Pete nods while gently placing the pistol in Prior's outstretched palm.

Prior waits through an uncomfortable silence before continuing. "Peter, I am afraid my hearing is not what it used to be at this advanced age. I said, are we clear?"

"Are we clear?" re-Pete repeats. "Yes."

"Excellent." Prior pockets the pistol and looks at the crucifixion tables. "I would certainly hate to see your talent go to waste."

# 63

"I can tell you grew up in the 'burbs," he says as we climb out of the car. He's not happy with the parking spot I picked.

"How?" I ask. It's a couple hours later so the concrete should be hard enough. So now we're walking up the street chatting like a couple of coworkers and not like a pair of semi-immortal wackjobs wrecking infrastructure as part of an effort to save themselves and others from an eternal hell of dying, because, you know, that would be weird.

"Where I grew up, we didn't have yards. I always expected, if I walked across someone's yard, some crazy old guy would come out and wave a gun at me, call me a whippersnapper or something. That's what I'm still picturing right now, like I'm looking at these houses and I'm nervous and you act like this is perfectly normal. That's how I can tell you grew up on a street like this."

"Well, it isn't just familiarity. Taking that thing on a dirt road would attract attention," I say, pointing over my shoulder at the tiny car. Which is true enough; no need to add I picked that particular parking spot to check on something.

We reach Muffin Man's house, and I'm disappointed to see his car still sitting in the driveway, the pastries still sitting on the hood. Maybe he doesn't like muffins, or maybe he's out of town. Or maybe I'm just setting myself up for disappointment with this expectation of acknowledgment, but whatever the case may be, the rain is going to pick up again soon enough. And when it does, those pastries are going to turn into a soggy mess. Maybe I should open the package so birds will at least have something to eat.

But then if the birds poop all over his car, that'll turn my gesture of gratitude into an act of vandalism, and then I'm going to owe him more muffins and a car wash, and I don't even know where to find a good car wash in this...

"You don't think maybe standing in someone's yard could attract the wrong kind of attention too?" I hadn't even noticed I'd stopped moving. I march him past the car and through the yard, worried he'll ask about the muffins. But the last thing he wants to do is linger.

It only takes us a couple minutes in the creek to screw the cap onto the end of the PVC pipe and finish sealing the tunnel. Santo takes an invisible notebook out of his pocket and starts checking items off an imaginary list. "Steal a cement truck from an unmarked graveyard? Check. Crawl through a storm tunnel? Check. Seal off said storm tunnel? Check."

"Wait for rain?" I say. I look up at the overcast sky and blink just as a raindrop splashes onto my eyeball.

"Check," Santo says while crossing that item off his list. We start moving back up the bank toward the car as more raindrops begin to fall. Santo leafs through a few more pages in his imaginary notebook as we walk, then looks at me with that same grim expression he used to wear whenever he'd murder me. "Now all that's left to do is die."

If that were all, it'd be easy. But we're about to attack a building full of mercenaries and at least two other people like us, people who don't stay dead. So we're going to attack and die and attack again, they're going to defend and die and defend again, and it's going to be like Cady's ex-boyfriend in the coffee shop times ten. And even if we do manage to pull it off, that's still only half the battle. I still so desperately want to run away.

I try to force my mind onto other things, like how I need to get some rest before I die so I can die and feel rested again. And how the muffins are still there on the hood of the car as we walk past it. We get to our little punchline of a car as the rain starts to pick up.

"Wanna grab a bite before we sleep?" Santo asks.

I nod and point the car toward downtown. Nice thing about driving at this time of day is no traffic. But there's no traffic because everyone already found their spot, so I drop Santo off at the first place he sees. He shoulders his bag full of guns and marches inside while I circle around in the rain looking for a place to park.

And then I see something familiar out of the corner of my eye, and someone familiar beyond it. The familiar thing is a sheet of paper stapled to a utility pole with a picture of me and a bunch of tear-off tabs. The familiar someone, well, if it is who I think it is, I should be getting out of here as fast as possible. But there's something about the way he's just sitting there oblivious to the wet and cold world around him that makes me circle back around the block.

I come back around, and sure enough, it's Grazi. He's sitting on a bench at a covered bus stop, looking up at the rain like it's whispering the meaning of life. There's something about the expression on his face that I can't look away from, he just looks so serene. And lost.

"Grazi!" I call his name, but he doesn't notice. I try a couple more times, and I know I'm loud enough, but nothing registers. It's like he doesn't recognize his name.

I pull over in front of a fire hydrant, grab my bag of guns, and walk over to him. "Hey. Grazi?" He looks my way without really seeing me, like he's looking for the source of the noise that's getting closer to him. I start to reach into my bag while looking for movement or any sense of awareness. There's a feeling you get in combat when you look around and realize that everyone is far away from you but all their eyes are on you because they all know something's about to happen, and it's the most frightening feeling I've ever felt before today. But no one's looking at me and I'm still feeling it.

In fact, what I'm experiencing right now is way more terrifying than walking into an ambush. I can hear my heartbeat in my ears, feel my pulse in my trigger finger as it finds its place in one of the many instruments of death in my backpack. I slowly approach until I'm standing in front of Grazi before he finally meets my eyes, which he only does for a second before focusing on the space above and beyond me. I know he's just looking at the sky, but I can't help myself from checking over my shoulder.

When I look back at Grazi, he's smiling, a wet spot blossoming on the front of his jeans as he pisses himself. I wait and watch this for a few painful seconds while he finishes. Then he looks at me again, his head cocked to the side. He holds his hand out, palm up like he's asking for something, or offering something.

"Piece, ah. Peat's, uh. Pizza! PIZZA!" he says.

I back away. Slowly at first, away from Grazi and away from re-Pete's illegally parked car toward the utility pole with my face on it. By the time I get there I'm running; I grab a tab and sprint across the street to a liquor store with a payphone out front. If I'd made better choices in life, I probably wouldn't even notice this vestige of yesteryear. I'd have a phone of my own in my pocket, and it wouldn't even occur to me that the item doubles as a tracking device.

I lift the receiver on the payphone, fumble in some coins, and dial the number on the tab. A voice picks up. Not the one I was hoping for, but it's the one I was expecting.

"Hello?" says Prior.

"What did you do?" I ask.

"Ah, Kenny. I am so glad I kept this phone by my desk as it would appear I have now won a bet with Peter. He was adamant that you would never make the mistake of calling this number again, but as I believe I mentioned once before, you have a mind very much like my own. It would be reasonable, therefore..."

I slam the receiver down in midsentence and spin around, looking for a way out. But a cop is pulling up next to re-Pete's illegally parked car. If I run back to the car, I'm screwed. If I run away, I'm screwed. Either way, I'll probably have to reset myself. My best option is to remain still, staring like a curious bystander. Cops don't look at those.

The phone rings behind me. I ignore it for a couple rings, but it's loud enough to reach the cop through the rain, who's just getting out of his car. And I recognize this one; he's not the sort of cop who issues parking tickets, he's the sort of cop who arrests people. Or kidnaps them.

I turn back around and pick up the phone before I'm made.

"...to presume I might guess your behaviors by asking what I myself might do, were I in your proverbial shoes," Prior continues as if he hadn't been interrupted.

"What did you do to him?"

"To whom?"

"Grazi."

"Ah, our funny friend. I could not stand the thought of our dear Grazi becoming our dead Grazi, but he had such a privileged position within our program and yet he wanted to leave! Can you believe that? I made him immortal, and he said he was sick and tired of dying. So, I asked him to participate in one final experiment before his departure."

"You killed him."

"Oh, that is not the case at all, a part of him is still very much alive, as you very well know. And it is for the best, I should think. You see Kenny, ours is a rather inconvenient immortality, wouldn't you agree? I believe I finally have a solution to this little one-day-at-a-time problem, but I am in desperate need of a very certain sort of mind. I hoped that your lady friend might be the right candidate, but alas, she became just another lab rat..."

I hang up again and reach into my bag, a gun in hand, ready to reset myself as I turn around. But the cop is too absorbed with reading the VIN number under the windshield.

So, I start walking away, my head to the side, keeping the cop in my peripheral vision until I'm down the block and around the corner.

When he sees me, Santo looks like he's about to open his mouth and say something. Then he does a subtle double take, reads the look on my face and silently follows me for a few blocks.

Once I think we're far enough away, I turn and explain. "That cop who picked me up outside the coffee shop, he got the car."

"How'd you get out?" he asks, looking over his shoulder, suddenly not convinced we've gone far enough.

“I wasn’t in it. You remember a guy by the name of Grazi?”

“Graziano? Yeah, I interviewed him. Was he looking for you?”

“He wasn’t even able to look at me. Wouldn’t have recognized his own mother.” I explain how and why I pulled over, adding some detail from the last time I saw Grazi, when he was strapped to one of Prior’s execution tables.

“Damn. That’s not good.”

“What did they do to him?”

Santo looks off into space for a second before answering. “ECT, Electro Convulsive Therapy. It’s used to treat extreme depression. Most people, when they try to commit suicide, if they fail, they never try again. The ones who do, you give them ECT in small doses, it rewires them. In large doses, it’s basically an electric lobotomy.”

“So wait. What? Why did Prior go from burying people to lobotomizing them?”

We turn a corner and Santo pauses under an awning. I stand with him, out of the rain.

"When I put the electrodes on you, there was a little bit of electrical current in them. You didn't feel it because I didn't turn it up, but it was built into the machine because Ethan knew he was going to go through a lot of bodies. The original plan was to wipe their minds and dump them downtown, but a hundred nameless morons start showing up, that'll create a trail. If it takes cops a week to follow that trail back to Prior and Prior can only go back a day when he resets, he's just painting himself into a corner. So he went with the construction plan instead. But if he's doing this now, it means he thinks he's close."

"He just said he's in desperate need of a certain kind of mind."

"Whoa. You spoke with him?"

"I called Cady's cell from a pay phone and Prior picked up. Said he's close to solving his 'little one-day-at-a-time problem.'"

"Oh, man. Kenny. We don't have a lot of time."

"Why, what does that mean?"

"It means he's found a way to go back further. He won't just wake up hours before us. He'll wake up days before us. Weeks, maybe."

# 65

Someday, if they ever make a movie out of this, I hope they don't make me out like some clichéd, combat-hardened veteran who gets dragged back into action because he has a unique skillset. But I also hope my skillset is actually unique, because we're about to go up against actual combat-hardened veterans, and if they can transcend death like I can this is going to be a long night.

We picked up a new crowbar yesterday since I left the old one in re-Pete's car, then we walked in the rain back to the cement truck where we spent half the night napping in the cab. Then we exhausted another half hour hiking over here. Now I'm cold, wet, and tired, and that gives me a warm and fuzzy feeling. Not because it reminds me of being a soldier, but because it reminds me of what it's like to have something to live for. And because I have a feeling our plan is going to work this time. One of these times.

"Ready?" Santo asks. I nod while tucking the crowbar under my left arm so I can check the chamber of the gun in my right hand. We're standing at the top of the parking lot, just beyond the motion sensors, each of us sporting a backpack full of guns while looking down the slight incline at the Prior Institute. The parking lot is a puddle, and that puddle has grown all the way up to the bullet-resistant sliding glass doors as we'd hoped it would. If that doesn't short the motor and unlock the sucker, I don't know what will.

"Are you ready?" Santo asks again, like a teenager about to take a test. He's more nervous than I am. Or maybe he's just colder and wetter. Whatever; after everything we've been through together and in spite of everything he's done to me, I don't have to get into his head to empathize. He needs some reassurance, so I give it to him.

"I'll meet you back at the truck," I say. It's not as witty as I wanted it to be, but the things we say through the adrenaline rarely ever are. It's enough to make him smile, at least.

We start sprinting into the parking lot, hitting our makeshift pond just as the alarm goes off. The water's deep enough to slow us down, but we just lift our legs and stomp rather than stride through it.

The lobby lights up just as we reach the door but those lights are part of the security system; there's no one in the vestibule yet. I jam the tip of the crowbar into the tiny space between the two thick slabs of glass and yank back with my left arm and all my might. And the sucker opens right up and slams into its slot in the wall.

We splash our way right into the lobby, waving our guns at all the nothingness that we see. It's empty, for now. I can't believe we made it this far, this has been the easiest...

# 66

BAM! My eyes slam open to the sound of Santo's wristwatch alarm going off. We're back in the cab of the cement truck. He turns the alarm off in a smooth practiced motion.

"Those guys move fast," Santo says.

"I don't think whoever got us was moving. There was a sentry somewhere. Did you get a look behind the guard desk?"

"Yeah, nothing."

"The dormitory door, then."

We go over our next plan for a couple minutes then get out into the rain and hike back to the building, and this time we don't stop to trade nervous assurances. We sprint into the parking lot and stomp through the big puddle to the door, which I yank open just as before.

We immediately split up, Santo diving for cover behind the guard desk, me running to the side of the dormitory door. It opens just a crack, just a second later, the barrel of a rifle protruding.

I grab the handle and yank it open to the surprise of the guy behind it. He's so unprepared he doesn't even flinch when I slam the crowbar into his cranium a fraction of a second later. I step to the side, even though I know the doorjamb isn't going to protect me from rifle rounds, and I aim my little pistol down the hall, but there's nobody there. They thought one guard would be enough because, well. A hidden guy with a high-powered rifle usually is.

"We need to keep moving!" Santo shouts while I zip tie the hands of the unconscious guard behind his back.

Just then, the door to the basement lab slams open and three more mercenaries explode out into the lobby. I hit the ground as round after round slams into the wall behind me; there's too much smoke and noise in the air, I can't see enough to know where to go, but from the sound of things I'm pretty much pinned down.

When all the sound and smoke clears, I see Santo standing next to almost three dead mercenaries. They're not almost dead, they're just almost all there, minus some face and brains. Looks like Santo managed to shoot them all in the head from behind as they were crossing the lobby toward my position.

"That's how you do it!" he shouts.

I want to say that's how they do it too, but I'm distracted by a glimpse of movement in the main entrance.

# 67

BAM! My eyes slam open to the sound of Santo's wristwatch alarm penetrating my brain. He turns it off then turns to me.

"Why'd you cuff him, Kenny?"

"So he wouldn't come to and come after us."

"OK, look. I agree, you need to neutralize him. But we can't afford to spend that much time on one man. We're at war."

I'm suddenly reminded of a time when I stopped to perform first aid on an enemy combatant, and a soldier next to me remarked that from that point on, he was going to eliminate that hassle by eliminating the wounded. As if he were doing me a favor.

When people talk about the horror of war, this is what they're really getting at. It's not just fear and death and violence, it's the million-and-one iterations of the underlying argument that got us there in the first place, and it's how we learn to use that argument against our enemies first and each other later, when we come home. "Santo, let me tell you something about war. War is not a failure of diplomacy, it's a triumph of persuasion. Not that it's better to kill than to be killed, but that human life has less value than resources or ideas. I've lost friends who were persuaded by that argument to enemies who were persuaded by that argument, so I hope you understand I'm not criticizing your position when I tell you mine, but I also hope you understand that I. Will not. Be persuaded."

I can see how much he wants to argue. And he can see how little that's going to accomplish. A long, tense moment passes. Then he throws his hands up in frustration. “Fine. Cuff ‘em. Where’d they come from this time, anyway?”

“The parking lot.”

“Huh. The rooftop shooters.”

“Yeah. All three doors. Only side they’re not coming from is the wall behind the security desk.”

“We both go behind the desk, then.”

“Two of us, three directions. We hole up there and we aren’t flanked, we’re surrounded.”

“Then what?”

My style of fighting has always been to lure someone into a trap and hit them when they don’t expect it, and now is no different. “We flank the flanking flankers.” I tell him my plan and I think he likes it almost enough to get over his butthurt about my pacifism. He likes it enough to start moving again, at least.

We get out into the rain and hike back to the building, sprinting once we reach the top of the parking lot. But we split up as soon as we hit the puddle, Santo taking position behind one of the mercenaries' rental cars while I rip open the left side of the door and enter, leaving the right side in place.

I head straight over to the dormitory door and surprise the guy behind it, but I don't wait to cuff him this time before running back across the lobby and diving behind the guard desk. Just a fraction of a second later, the door to the basement lab slams open and three more guards come rushing out. I throw a few rounds over the top of the desk, not to neutralize them but to send them seeking cover.

Two more guards enter through the main entrance, but their faces disintegrate into a spray of blood and brains just as soon as they cross the threshold. Santo emerges a moment later to stand in front of the right-hand slab of bullet-resistant glass. He reaches around and throws a couple shots into the room to draw fire, then withdraws his arm just before the shooters oblige him. He stands there dancing in front of the door as round after round hits the glass, but nothing penetrates and they keep firing in a state of confusion and rage until they're empty.

Then I come out from behind the desk, a gun in each hand, and start firing as fast and low as I can. I feel bad about shredding their legs like this, but not as bad as they're going to feel when it's over.

Once they're down and screaming, Santo steps inside to cover the doors with his guns and me with his impatient glare while I tourniquet the mercenaries' legs with zip ties. Then I cuff the guy behind the door. And just like that, we have rifles.

We race across the lobby to the basement door; Santo shoulders me aside, I'm guessing to eliminate anyone coming up the stairs before I can inconvenience him by wounding them, but we make it down the stairwell without encountering anybody.

But we encounter plenty of bodies in the hallway. They're alive and walking, their numbers slowly increasing as more and more of them pour out of the door at the other end of the hall, but these aren't guards. Judging from their lack of shoes and the lack of uniformity in their clothing, they're civilians. And judging from the lack of presence behind their eyes, we're too late. They all have that same meandering, empty gaze that I last saw in Grazi.

The last few bodies emerge from the door to the lab, followed by Prior, re-Pete, and two guards in black surplus BDUs.

"Ah, there you are Santo," Prior says. "I knew it was only a matter of time before you would return. And my dear Kenny! So good to see you again! Santo, thank you for bringing him back to me."

Santo raises his rifle and the guards on either side of Prior and re-Pete respond in kind. I want to warn Santo that they aren't waiting for him to shoot, they're just waiting for any indication that he's about to. But I can't stop staring at the mindless civilians packing the hallway between us. "I didn't bring him here for you," Santo says.

I get a deep, sick feeling in my gut when I recognize one of the civilians in the hallway. It's the Muffin Man.

"Oh, my dear boy, if I somehow led you to the mistaken conclusion that I was attempting to drive a wedge between you and your friend, I do apologize. I am merely grateful that the two of you, my two favorite former employees, should return in time to witness my success. We have made so many strides, and so many sacrifices." He gestures with his arms at the wave of bodies between us. "But your timing is impeccable, as I believe we are ready for this final phase."

The Muffin Man looks at me like he's trying to remember where he's seen me before, but that moment lasts all of about a second before his eyes wander with that same look to the person next to him, and then to the next one and the next one after that. I'm wrestling with a sick feeling in my gut while scanning the crowd for Cady.

"How are you going to get rid of this many bodies?" Santo asks.

I see everything, and it's too much to take in. Prior, re-Pete, the armed guards with their fingers on the triggers, the mindless civilians, the door with scuff marks on the frame from my boots. But I don't see Cady.

"Ah my dear Santo, asking the wrong question as usual. This has always been your greatest shortcoming, don't you know. How is irrelevant. To need or not to need, that is the question. You see, very soon I will not need to 'get rid of any bodies,' as it were."

"You need to stop," Santo says while closing his left eye so he can sight down the rifle with his right. The guards on either side of Prior and re-Pete don't visibly react to this, but I know they're taking a breath and adding a pound of pressure to their triggers. Any second now, one of them is going to exhale and put a round through Santo's amygdala. Or his leg. Or one of the mindless civilians standing in the way.

If the shooting begins, a lot of these people are going to die. And they're Resets, but they lack the awareness to ever find a way out of this hallway. If they die in here, they will spend eternity in here dying.

Out of the corner of my eye I see Santo's finger going white on the trigger. I turn and jump on his rifle just as he completes a pull of the trigger, knocking it down and to the side. A bullet slams into the floor and fragments. Some of the Resets look alarmed. The Muffin Man looks down at his leg and the shrapnel from Santo's floor shot embedded in it.

"Ow," he says as he crumbles to the floor.

And then the guards start firing, mowing down men between us. A bunch of bullets tear into me, I can't count how many. Santo shakes me off as I fall to the ground; he raises his rifle again and gets a couple shots off, but he's being riddled with bullets while he does this, so all he succeeds in doing is killing some more civilians.

I can't hear anything through the ringing in my ears, and everything I see flashes past like I'm looking at it through the windows of a moving train. I don't want to look forward because I'm entering a tunnel, and I know there's no light at the end of this one.

I look to one side and see what's left of Santo lying face-down on the ground, his blood forming a puddle around him. To my other side, I see what looks like a mountain approaching me. Something moves me; I feel it more than I see it, but as I squint into the fading light around me, that mountain materializes into re-Pete's face.

He's crying, and for the first time in all the many times I've ever looked into his eyes, I'm not afraid. Because I recognize that look; every time I tried to save a life and failed, every person who's died in my care, whether I loved or hated them, knew them or not, I felt the feeling I'm seeing on re-Pete's face.

I'm not afraid because, as I look into his eyes, I see myself staring back.

"I'm sorry," he says.

# 68

Well, that's not what I was expecting.

My eyes open to the sound of Santo's alarm going off. That feeling of waking up after dying is always so sudden and shocking, but this time, I can't help but wonder for a moment whether I even died. Or whether I'm even alive. I might be just imagining these things. There are a lot of things I might just be imagining.

"What the hell was that about?" Santo asks as he turns to me.

"Re-Pete doesn't want to kill us."

"What? You blocked my shot and got us killed because you think he's a pacifist? He's got the moral high ground now? News flash Kenny, I've taken dumps with more moral fiber than that guy!"

"He apologized. He meant it."

"Oh yeah, I'm sure he's real sorry. Hey, here's an idea, how about you not jump on my gun next time, huh? Then maybe we can take a turn at not getting shot to hell and you can be the one who apologizes for winning. You think that'd feel good? I bet that'd feel real good."

I slowly turn and meet his eyes. And for just a moment, I feel like I can look past his pupils into the neural network behind them and see all the patterns that make up his personality, the constellations that comprise his potential, and the beliefs that compromise it. I'm like Prior watching someone's life scroll down the screen, except unlike Prior, I want to use what I know to save him. Or maybe it's just myself I'm trying to save.

"Ground control to Major Kenny," Santo says.

He thinks we're fighting to save ourselves from an evil genius, two guards, and a room full of zombies. Those two guards probably think they're fighting to protect an old doctor and a room full of mental patients from us. Everyone thinks they're right, which is why everyone's willing to fight, which is how I know everyone is wrong. But where does re-Pete fit into all this?

"Kenny?" Santo's starting to look alarmed now. Every time he inhales he takes in a little more than he lets out. This is a vestigial survival instinct, an involuntary reaction to fear that makes him look bigger while giving him more oxygen to draw from, but it also puts tension into his back and shoulders, and that tension stokes the fear.

"Did they get you on one of those tables before you reset?" he asks. That's right, he died before I did, so he didn't see what I saw. And all he sees now is me staring back at him the same way Grazi stared back at me a few hours and as many lifetimes ago.

And just like that, I come crashing back into his reality. "I'm fine," I say, shaking my head to clear it.

He exhales so hard it throws him into a coughing fit. When he finally settles, he opens the door and leans out to spit. The interior light comes on, bathing him in a sick yellow glow. "Man, for a second there, you were starting to remind me of those people in the hall."

"I recognized one of those people."

He shuts the door and looks at his reflection in the window, and for a second, his reflection blinks back at him with eyes full of pain and regret. Then the interior light times out and his reflection disappears with it. But he just keeps on staring into the darkness on the other side of the glass. "Imagine what it would be like to recognize all of them. To look into a room full of people like that and remember spending time with each of them, interviewing them one-by-one, reassuring them that they're going to get better while you're putting the electrodes on them."

"You knew them all?"

"Not from that batch, no."

"You can't kill them."

He turns back to me with a defiant look that I know all too well; he's determined to do what he's decided is the right thing to do. "I can't save them. But I can save the next batch after them, and the next one after that," he says.

This isn't a matter of right or wrong, it's just another one of those arguments we use on our enemies first and each other later. I call this one the transitive property of morality: two wrongs may not make a right, but a big enough wrong on one side of the equal sign should cancel out the wrong on the other side. And the thing is, it works on paper and in the history books. But it's the kind of equation you write with a blowtorch.

"Santo, human shields aren't there to make you feel conflicted. They're there to absorb bullets. And the guys behind them have more bullets and better aim. We can't go through them."

"We have no choice. They're in the way."

"There's always another way."

"OK, pacifist. What's your plan?"

"As soon as we hit the parking lot, that alarm goes off and everyone mobilizes. While we're dealing with the sentry in the dormitory and the guards coming up the stairs, the Resets are being marched out into the hallway. We think we have to go through them because they're there, because the sentry and the guards are slowing us down. There's no way around them, right?"

I fish into my pocket, pull out the key to my own private hell and show it to him. "There is. We just have to be fast."

# 69

We fine tune the plan a bit and then get moving, with our fifty-pound bags of steel and lead between us and another twenty thousand pounds of metal under our asses.

We hiked in the last few times because there are only so many places where you can park a cement truck without drawing attention. It's rented in the name of the Prior Institute, so if we were to leave it under a no-parking sign outside or on a residential street near the facility someone might come knocking on the driver's side door. Or worse, they might call the cops. And we couldn't leave it in the parking lot either, we'd eat up too much time stopping and parking and disembarking.

But if we park it inside the building, not only do we arrive rested and dry, we also have a whole new door to work with. And it's amazing what a difference just a few minutes and twenty tons of metal can make.

I don't like this plan. Not because it's bad, but because it puts Santo in charge of the guards. But at least it'll save the Resets, and then who knows? Maybe while we're figuring a way out of our little immortality problem, we can figure out a way to help them too. Maybe I'll also get a chance to ask re-Pete a couple questions. The thought of talking to him terrified me before, but I'm less afraid of him now.

I shake my head to clear it as Santo clears the last couple streets, coming to a stop about a block from the building. I open the passenger-side door and look out into the rain and darkness. Then I look back at the first man who ever murdered me. I've got such a heavy feeling in my chest right now and I don't know why. But he's smiling. And it's go time.

"See you in a few minutes or a few minutes ago," he says.

I swivel my legs out, let myself fall, and hit the ground running. Santo revs the engine behind me as he wrestles it into first gear, and just as I reach the parking lot, he passes me, slowing only enough to make the turn, doing his best not to lose momentum.

He floors it and starts picking up speed as we trigger the alarm and the lights come on. A few seconds later, while I'm still stomping through a puddle, he jumps out into the water and grass and mud. And just about a second after that, the truck slams into the side of the building, creating a gaping hole right around where the dormitory door and sentry are. Or were.

I don't stop to see whether he made it out of the truck intact or into the building; for this plan to work, we can't afford to lose a second.

I hear shots going off as I get to the sliding glass doors. I hook the tip of the crowbar between them, and slam open the left side before jumping back behind the right. I drop the crowbar and get a gun in each hand, but I know better than to expose myself to the guards coming up the stairs. The only reason I had an advantage over them before was because their backs were to me.

They come pouring out the door to the basement lab a second later and get a dozen or more shots into the door in about the amount of time it takes me to flinch. The door still holds, at least for now. I think Santo and I managed to unload a couple hundred rounds into this door before, but those weren't from high-powered assault weapons; these guys are using civilian versions of the same rifle I carried in deployment, so those are thirty-round magazines. If they start firing again, I doubt they'll have to reload before the door dissolves.

And I think they know that from the way they're spreading out into the room. They glance around, one set of eyes on me while the other two examine the hole in the wall with the crumpled front of the cement truck intruding through it. I fire a shot into the ground next to me to draw their attention, and am rewarded as they dismiss the empty truck to take up positions to cover each other so one can fire and then reload while another one fires.

Just as they start shooting, Santo appears behind them, a gun in each hand. The first two go down fast. The one in the middle notices his friends falling before he realizes that some of the shots fired didn't come from his colleagues, but by then, it's too late. He starts to do a one-eighty but Santo annihilates him before he can complete sixty of those degrees.

I'm running through the lobby before his body hits the ground. I pocket one gun and fumble around it in my pocket for the key while racing down the stairs into the hallway to hell, reaching the door with the scuff marks on either side. I get the key out of my pants, into the door knob, and I manage to turn it while turning around so I can make sure I wasn't seen while I quietly step backward inside. Every step of this plan has been tight, but getting into this room quickly and closing the door without a sound has been the hardest part. And I think I pulled it off.

I keep my eyes and ears on the door, and am rewarded a moment later by the sound of shuffling footsteps outside. I get down on my knees and put my cheek on the cold tile floor so I can peek through the crack under the door. I see a lot of feet, most of them bare. And then I see a pair of running shoes, which I recognize as belonging to re-Pete, followed by a pointy pair of oxfords and two sets of tactical boots. They're heading toward the lobby to create a bottleneck of bodies while simultaneously giving themselves more space to fall back on, should they need it. It's a sound tactic, except in just a moment, as soon as I hear Santo's voice, I'm going to step out behind them.

Soon as I hear Santo's voice, I think to myself as I stand up, step back, and slip on something. I manage to turn around and regain my balance without falling or making a sound, but then I realize what I'd slipped on was blood.

And then I see the girl on the floor. She's been shot to pieces in a crude attempt at torture, her limbs utterly mutilated, unconscious and slipping away, but still alive. Barely.

It's Cady.

"Ethan Prior, I'm here to put a stop to your experiment!" Santo shouts in the corridor behind me.

That cheesy line is supposed to be my cue, but I can't move. I can't even think about moving. All I can think about is how she's dying, how she'll die over and over again, and I can't do anything to save her. It's like I'm back on the battlefield watching my friend, waiting for his head to explode.

"Santo, my dear friend, I am afraid you are out of your depth," Ethan's voice says in the hallway behind me.

Soon, sooner than now even, she'll wake up and go through it all again and again. And I can't even pick up my weapon. There's no point even trying, I'm too late to save her.

"You know how they say you are what you eat? Well, eat death!" Santo shouts from a world away.

Shots are fired in the hall behind me, but I don't even flinch. I can hear some of the Resets panicking, running around, running into walls. A couple of them even run into the door behind me. I think I can hear a couple bodies falling to the floor, punctuating Santo's screams. He's been hit, but he's still screaming, which means they're taking him alive.

There's some more commotion, followed by the sound of Santo being dragged across the floor. I know it's Santo because the sound of his voice gets louder with the sound of the body being dragged, then it fades away as they drag him past my door to the lab. He's screaming my name, begging, pleading with every inch and ounce of energy left in him, but I can't move.

All I can do is stand here and watch as Cady's last breath leaves her body.

# 70

Minutes pass. Hours, maybe. I've lived entire lifetimes shorter than this, but every minute in this hell feels like an eternity.

I'm awakened from my nightmare by a knock on the door.

"Kenny?" Prior's voice.

I open the door and step out into the hallway because I have nowhere else to go. Prior's standing just a few feet away, leaning on his cane, with re-Pete by his side. Re-Pete's holding a gun in one hand. I had a gun in each of mine, but I don't know where they are. I had a bag full of guns but I think I left them in the room behind me.

"Tell me Kenny, were you with Santo when you awoke this morning?" Prior asks.

I nod.

"I am sure it will please you to know that our friend is alive and well," he looks toward the lab, "although he has forgotten his name. So tell me, Kenny, would you like me to reset you right now?"

I don't nod.

"No? Afraid to go it alone? Or would you rather reset yourself, is that it?" He looks at re-Pete. "Peter, why don't you give Kenny the gun?"

Re-Pete looks at Prior with alarm. "What? He'll kill me."

"I think not. And I think it is time you learned yet another lesson. Peter, give Kenny the gun."

Re-Pete just stands there, sweating. Prior rolls his eyes and continues. "You must forgive me Kenny, I misled you. You see, Peter actually does not possess the same gift I gave you. I needed someone with sufficient motivation to do what he was told, which meant I needed him to retain a healthy fear of dying. And he has been an absolutely stellar employee until just recently. Peter has been misbehaving of late, feeding the test subjects, failing to meet his recruitment goals... he even suspected you might be hiding in there, but he did not reveal this to me. Which is why he must learn a lesson, which is why, Peter, you will give Kenny your gun. Right. Now."

After a moment, re-Pete offers me the gun, his hand trembling.

"There is only one bullet left in that weapon, Kenny. What will you do? Kill Peter? Reset me? Or reset yourself so that you return alone, without your friend?"

I just look at the gun in re-Pete's hand; I won't touch it. And by the smile on Prior's face, he knows this.

He steps forward, snatches the gun and points it at re-Pete's head. And pulls the trigger.

Click!

Re-Pete falls to his knees, feeling his head for a wound. Then he looks at Prior.

"Is there anything you have to say to me, Peter?"

"Is there anything I have to say to you?" he asks. And it occurs to me, in this moment, that I've been to war and I've been homeless but I've never seen a man so defeated. "Yes, there is. Thank you."

Satisfied, Prior turns to me. "Kenny, I thought I knew you. Despite your many shortcomings, I had rather high expectations, and therein, I now realize, lies my folly. I saw in you a mind much like my own, and in doing so I projected onto you what I wanted to see while failing to realize just how incredibly useless you are."

He suddenly swings his cane in an explosive arc that begins with the floor and ends in my shoulder. Pain shoots up my neck and down into my arm. He takes another swing but misses as I back away. He looks like he wants to hit me again but he's already winded. Whether by his actions or the rage behind them, I can't tell. I'm too busy running.

"Peter! Bring that subject back here and put it where it belongs!" He screams as I run to the stairwell, up the steps and out into the lobby, past the blood and bodies, through the front door into the cold, wet puddle that was a parking lot.

I run out into the street and just keep running because it's all I know how to do.

# 71

BAM! The dumpster lid goes down like a gunshot and I open my eyes to the painful realization that I'll never sleep forever.

Then I look around and remember where I am. I ran until I found myself back in that same old alley behind the Michelin-rated restaurant with the signature saffron marsala sauce and the pasta plates that no one ever seems to finish. If I look up, I'll see the old familiar face of another loser like me. It'll be like looking into a mirror. I don't want to look up.

"Shit," Meatball says.

He started to tell me something once that stuck in my mind, but I didn't stick around to listen. I was too busy trying to kickstart my life while saving one someone and running from another someone who was trying to save me. They're both gone now. All that's left from that weird day is a guy named after a sandwich.

"Shit?" he asks.

"My name's Kenny."

"Well, you look like Shit," he says, laughing.

I get it. If I were in his shoes, I'm sure I'd find that hilarious. But right now, all I want to do is be in his shoes. Or anyone else's.

I finally turn and meet his eyes. "Can I ask you something?"

He looks me up and down, shrugs, and takes a seat next to me.

"Usually, when someone wants to ask me something, they look like you," he says. "And usually, what they wanna ask has something to do with finding drugs. They see a homeless man and assume that's what he knows, a homeless man sees them and assumes that's what they want. It's hard to really see people when we already think we know what we're going to see. But if you can see me enough to ask, I can see you enough to answer."

Touché; I didn't think he was worth a second glace, when I first met him. "Last time I saw you, you said I was starting to see through the illusion."

"Yeah, I remember."

"What's the illusion?"

"How much time you got?"

"This isn't one of those things where you're going to translate some ancient text, is it?"

"No, this is one of those things that don't translate. No word in the English language describes it. Don't get me wrong, people try, but what you're dealing with at this level is basically synonyms between languages, and nothing is perfectly synonymous even before you start treating a word from one language like it's a definition in another. If I give you the translation, it's gonna be a bad one."

"OK, well, give me the bad one."

"Attachment."

"I'm attached to something? That's my problem?"

"No, that's your illusion, that you even ask what you're attached to instead of what's your attachment. I told you it was a bad translation, 'cause it implies if someone breaks your heart, being attached to people is the problem. Someone steals your car, being attached to things is the problem. You get homesick, being attached to places is the problem. But this thing we call attachment, it isn't being stuck, it's the stickiness. It isn't the itch, it's the urge to scratch."

"So what if I have an urge to stay alive?"

"So what if you do, how long you think you're gonna pull that off? Life doesn't mean anything without death, we don't have a word for one without the other. Some people spend their whole lives trying to run away from the thing that made them alive in the first place. Then they die, and that's tragic. Not that they died, but that they never lived."

"What do I do if someone's trying to kill me? Give up and embrace death? Buy a motivational poster?"

"That's your attachment talking. There's always another option, but you're not going to see it until you see what's going on inside yourself first. Then, maybe, you can recognize the attachment in others and help them overcome it, because that's what happens when you handle your own attachment, you stop working against everyone and start working with them. I call it people skills, but it's everything you're up against skills, I mean if I was up against lions I'd call it lion skills. Come face-to-face with a lion, you're gonna taste every flavor of this thing we call attachment. You're gonna want to live, you're gonna be angry at the lion, then you're gonna realize you can't outrun it. Desire, aggression, and apathy, all in one bite. You get stuck in that, you're lion shit. But if you can get unstuck, you start to understand that the lion isn't your enemy, the lion is just hungry. And when you really understand that, that's when you're gonna come up with a solution."

Something clicks into place in the space between my ears. "That's how you got your name. You didn't tell them you needed a meatball sandwich. You told them *they* needed a meatball sandwich."

"And they did! They've been carrying it on their menu ever since!"

"How do I do that, how do I get unstuck?"

"You're here, right now, in this moment, but your mind is everywhere else." He picks up a rock and throws it at the dumpster. "That's the most amazing thing about your mind. It's also the most awful thing." He picks up another rock and chucks it against the side of the dumpster. Then he picks up another one and is about to throw it, but shows it to me instead. "Your mind can go backward and forward, and when it does, it isn't in the now, so whatever is happening now is just another one of hundreds of thoughts you can't handle. You can't even handle this moment, much less appreciate it. Like this, right now, this is just a rock hitting a bucket of trash. Right? But listen to it this time, and focus on the sound."

He throws the rock and it hits with a dull metallic thud that has a bit of a ringing sound like an auditory aftertaste that's actually kind of beautiful, as it fades away into the background noises of traffic and pigeons cooing. "It's different now because you're hearing it now, because you're here and now and not tripping in that time travel machine between your ears. That's what living really is. Easy enough, right?"

He picks up another rock, but this time, instead of throwing it at the dumpster, he throws it at my chest. It startles me. "Sure it is, until the next distraction. And the next one, and the next one after that. Takes work to be able to come back to the moment, it takes exercise. There's a Latin word for this exercise, another one of those words that don't translate perfectly. In one sense it means to measure, in another it means to contemplate. That word is 'Meditari.'"

"Wait, meditation? How is that going to help?"

"Do it for a while and find out."

"Is there another way?"

"Yeah, I hear dying also works."

"What you would say if I told you I've already died a bunch of times?"

"I'd say you suck at it. Come here." He scoots and shifts and turns around until he's facing the wall, and I join him. "Stare at the wall and think about your breathing," he says. "You don't think about breathing because you don't have to, your body handles that for you. But try thinking about it now, and when another thought pops into your head, acknowledge that thought, let it go, and come back to your breathing. See how long you can do that. It's harder than you think."

I try it, and boy is he wrong. I breathe, in and out, in and out, innie, outie. I wonder if people with innies get outies when they overeat.

"You're not thinking about your breathing right now, are you?" he asks.

Damnit, he's right. I lasted all of three breaths.

"So this is the trick," he says. "Your mind is gonna wander, and that's part of the exercise. This is an endurance exercise, but it isn't about how long you can go thinking about breathing, it's how long you can keep coming back to thinking about breathing when your mind keeps wanting to wander off. It's like doing chin ups. Don't do one and hold it, do the reps. Every time your mind wanders off, soon as you realize it, acknowledge the thought, decide you don't need to chase that thought, and let it go. Then come back to your breathing."

I do this for a few minutes. I think about breathing, I think about Santo, I let that go and come back to my breathing. I think about Prior, and then I come back to my breathing. I think about a bunch of things, and then I come back to my breathing a bunch of times. And I'm starting to feel better.

But then I think about Cady, and all of a sudden all I can do is picture her dead body, before I'm suddenly picturing all the other dead bodies I've ever seen. The mercenaries in the lobby, the resets in the hallway, frenemies and enemies alike on the battlefield. Everyone I've ever loved and lost, tried and failed to save. No matter how hard I try, I can't let this thought go, nor the feeling that goes with it. And it occurs to me, as I sit with this sick feeling of failure and regret gnawing at my guts, that the reason most of my life felt like hell was because I wasn't in it, or because my mind wasn't. But I still can't shake this feeling I've had forever already, this sick sense of fear and despair and of desperately wanting to be anywhere and anyone else.

"Don't fight it," I hear Meatball say beside me, and I realize my eyes were closed. I open them and stare at the wall and try to return to the moment and my breathing but I still can't push the thoughts and feelings away. "Kenny, lean into it. You can't let it go until you acknowledge it. Whatever it is, no matter how bad it is, recognize it. Accept it." I try with all my might to do as he says, but oh, it feels so bad.

But I stay with it, and after a few moments, it starts to fade and I manage to come back to my breathing. And after a few more moments, understanding washes over me like a tsunami: I wasn't attached to saving people, saving people was my attachment. It was how I dealt with the fear of losing people, and it got worse every time I lost someone, because I can't not lose people. But I realize now that I can lose the attachment, and in knowing this, I think I know what to do.

"Thank you," I say after what feels like a few lifetimes. And I know what a few lifetimes feel like. "I have just one more question."

He looks at me with a familiar look on his face, like he's going to go eat some trash and save the world, and it's a familiar face because I'm wearing that same one. It's like I'm looking into a mirror.

"What else I can do for you?"

"Do you know where I can find some drugs?"

# 72

My hands are shaking, my heart is racing, my guts feel like jello, and I'm going to die. I guess enlightenment doesn't last long.

Still, something's rubbed off on me, because if death is a lion, I'm not running from it anymore, and I'm not fighting it either. I'm marching right up to it, grabbing it by the teeth, and giving it a pet name.

But I just talked a homeless man who hates drugs into helping me score some and I don't want to think about that after the fact for the same reason I don't want to think about going to the bathroom when I'm not going to the bathroom because it's distracting me from what I should be thinking about which is what I'm doing next and what the hell is going on with re-Pete who acted like he hated me when I gave him every reason to but only because he gave me every reason to give him every reason every time he killed me but now I'm starting to realize he might be in the same mess I'm in or maybe I'm just overthinking… whoa.

I'm terrified, I'd rather be anywhere else, but I let that train of thought go and come back to my breathing. I savor the air after the rain and feel every step as I put one foot in front of the other and then I come back to my breathing. I realize I'm meditating while walking, and I think that's the coolest thing ever until I realize I'm not meditating anymore, and so I come back to my breathing. I think about how weird it is, that all I'm doing is letting go my thoughts and coming back to my breathing, and then I let that thought go and come back to my breathing.

I turn off the street into the parking lot that once was a puddle. There's a hole in the wall that we made with a truck, and the once-green lawn is now a soggy mess of mud and debris, but there's no puddle between my feet and the asphalt. And the rental cars are gone, and the alarm isn't going off, maybe because it's the middle of the day, or perhaps because Prior reached a point where he no longer needs security. It's just as well, I'm not really here to assault the building anyway. I'm here to work on my people skills.

I march right into the front door not knowing what to expect, but definitely expecting some sort of engagement; an alarm, guards, something. Anything. Instead all I see are a handful of workers cleaning up a mess I helped make by the dormitory door. I stop and watch them; if Prior's been pulling from the local population, these guys will be easy pickings. I want to tell them whatever you do don't go downstairs, your boss has a bad habit of turning people into vegetables, but I'm not sure anyone would listen to a warning like that.

I realize they've stopped working. I'm staring at them while they're staring at the door to the basement, where Re-Pete's is staring back at me. I meet his gaze; he has a familiar look in his eyes which I used to think was anger or hate or resentment or worse, but which I now recognize as fear. I can't believe I didn't see that for what it was when I first met him, all those many lifetimes ago.

"Can I ask you something?" I ask.

"You want to ask me something?"

"Yeah, why do you always repeat the question?"

I'm asking a man twice my size about his comprehension skills in front of a hole in a wall that I helped make while assaulting a facility that turns people into immortal morons, and the workers who are cleaning up my mess are just looking at us like this is the most awkward interaction ever. Maybe it is.

"You should go," he finally says.

"But," I start to say.

"No!" he cuts me off. "Any day now..." he glances around, unwilling to finish that sentence in front of witnesses, so he crosses the lobby. "Any minute now he's going to send me out after you. You had a head start! What are you doing here?"

He's standing just five feet away now, although he's so large and intimidating it feels like he's right on top of me. I feel that familiar fight or flight reflex that usually hits me right before he does, but this time, I don't avoid it. I don't fight it, either. I grab it by the teeth and give it a name.

"Peter," I say, using his real name for the first time. It's not a muffin, but it's not an insult, either. It's just enough to change the look on his face from fear to pain. "Peter, I remember things that you don't. Things you said in a past we don't share. I don't even know what to call that. Another dimension? Another time?"

"Time isn't even real, it's just a construct we use to measure intervals in causality." He launches himself into the explanation. "Like if you cut an orange in half, you think you have half an orange, right? But that fraction isn't the reality of the orange, the reality is the water and the sunlight and the soil and the seed. Time is just another way of looking at causality, which is why this Reset Paradox is so weird, because every time you reset, you're restarting reality, but the one you're leaving behind still exists in some dimension or some way or something, I don't even understand it all. That was the hardest thing for me to grasp when I started working here, that the linear universe is an illusion, and I don't mean an illusion in the colloquial sense, I mean..." He stops and just looks at me. "What, were you just expecting me to repeat the question?" he asks. And that's when I realize I'm staring at him with my mouth open.

"I'm sorry, I just. I didn't expect that. Why did you start working here? Are you an engineer?"

He shakes his head and smiles sadly. "I'm degreed in comparative literature, actually. But you have no idea how hard it is to find a job in my field when you look like me. I interviewed for teaching positions, but they all wanted me to coach sports. So I interviewed at libraries, but they thought I'd scare away children. At least I got used to being treated like a big dumb thug. That's how I learned to act like one."

"So that's why you repeat everything? To make people think you're dumb?"

"Dumb people don't have to make the hard decisions. Look, I know this isn't a moral argument, but this is my situation." He glances at the workers on the other side of the lobby. "It's bad enough being

Ethan's enforcer. If I had to make the decisions, I don't know that I could live with myself."

"Is there a way out?" My segue to asking how I can help, which is the question I came here to ask.

"Not that I can see. If I were to quit, Ethan would go after my family. If I were to kill myself, he'd just go back and stop me. I know because I tried. I picked up a gun, I knew it was loaded, but then it suddenly wasn't. Ethan reset himself just so he could go back and unload the gun. And not to move it, and not to talk to me, either, just to unload it. He let me try to kill myself so he could break me. He calls it 'teaching me a lesson.'"

"Thank you," I say.

"For what?"

"For trusting me. I think I can help you now, but first, mind if I take a nap?"

# 73

He didn't think I could handle Prior, but he let me in anyway. He was even nice enough not to put me in my old room so I wouldn't have to sit there with Cady's cadaver. In return, I politely refrained from leaving scuffmarks on the doorframe, and just like that a beautiful friendship has begun, the kind that will last until the day I die.

If I'm lucky, it'll last even longer, maybe a whole week.

Now begins the hard part. Because by now, a decision has been made; I'll either be left in here for longer than a person can stay awake or for longer than a person can stay alive. So my job right now is to keep my eyes open or die trying. Good thing Peter didn't frisk me, else he would have found enough crystal meth in my pockets to either keep me up for a week or pop my heart like a balloon. Or both.

I sit down on the cold tile floor and start practicing Meatball's meditation trick by paying attention to my breathing and allowing thoughts to pass through. After a few hours, when I can hardly keep my eyes open, I eat some meth and pace around the room until my teeth start to vibrate. Then I go back to meditating.

According to Peter, time is nothing more than measurement. And according to the guy I bought these crystals from, they last about four hours a pop. Which is helpful to know because it's the only way I have in here to mark the passage of time. Time may not be real, but exhaustion sure is. So is the humming in my teeth.

About halfway into my stash, the door opens and Peter steps inside. "Ethan is ready for you."

I get up slowly; my feet are numb, my back aches, and my eyes feel like they've been dipped in hot sauce. Peter gives me a glance and a moment to let the circulation back into my legs.

"You look like shit," he says.

I'm suddenly reminded of Meatball and I can't help but laugh. "Actually, my name is Kenny," I say once I'm finally able.

He looks over his shoulder like the joke just went over his head and crashed in the hallway behind him, then looks back at me. "He's going to get suspicious if we don't hurry."

"OK." I start moving. "How good an actor are you?"

He gives me his best blank stare and pulls a re-Pete. "How good an actor am I? Very."

We walk down the adjoining hallway and enter Prior's lab with me leading the way and Peter bringing up the rear like he's blocking my escape. And it occurs to me, for just a second, that he might be doing precisely that. I'm not sure whether this morbid fantasy is a habit from a lifetime of morbid fantasies or a side effect of methamphetamines, but as I look around the room and take in the familiar sight of the execution tables and the desk where Prior killed his first Reset, it's all I can do to not turn around and bolt.

I pay attention to my breathing instead, allowing that thought to pass. A moment later, I realize Prior's waiting for me to say something. "What?" I ask.

"I said I am very disappointed in you, Kenny, as it would seem that this time, I am the one to have lost a bet. Peter here said you would return on your own, did you not Peter?"

"Did I not? No, I did," Peter says in character.

"Indeed, your presence is a surprise Kenny, but a pleasant one nevertheless. As they say, if you love something, set it free."

"Yeah, I always wanted to be a boomerang when I grew up."

"Ah, how we missed your biting wit. Tell me, Kenny, to what do we owe this pleasure?"

"I wanted to ask. Did you ever figure out how to undo this Reset condition?"

He steeples his fingers and smiles. "Such a curious question. Did I ever figure out how to undo the greatest gift mankind will ever know? A discovery that will have a more profound impact on our species than anything we've yet to even imagine? The ability not to turn back time but to return from it? No, I have not yet figured out how to accomplish such a fatuous task, although perhaps I could have if I'd only been focusing on it."

"Then what have you been focusing on? Curing cancer?"

He gets up, leaning heavily on his cane. "Mock me if you must Kenny, but I happen to suffer from something much worse than cancer, a condition that takes far more lives than every other disease combined, one that is very much real and quite incurable. It is called age. What would you do if you were in my shoes, hmm? What would you do, Kenny, if you knew that you had squandered a lifetime doing anything other than seeking a cure for the condition that made this a lifetime in the first place?"

He points his cane at me like a pistol with a really long barrel and continues fiercely. "Nothing, is what you would do. Give up and die, is what you would do, but only because you are not me. I, on the other hand, have lived enough in this lifetime to crave another, because I have lived more than one lifetime in this. Since the day you and I met, nearly every conversation you have had with me, I have had many times over with you. While you were plotting and planning against me like a fly at a picnic, I was beating Death at a game of chess. Whereas you would have surrendered to the inevitability of your demise, I have redefined survival. Soon enough, I will be able to go back a week, a month, even more. I will go back to a point in time before you and I met and improve upon our first conversation and every one that followed. In fact I will do so repeatedly."

"How can you do that?"

"How indeed! It does my heart good that you ask the right question, although I fear the complexity of the answer might be beyond your intellectual reach. How did we annihilate Hiroshima and Nagasaki, for example? One might simply say we learned to split the atom, but such is the sort of answer a layperson only thinks they understand, and then only if they accepted it while they were very young, before their mind was fully developed. No, the answer is so much more elaborate, and one which does not translate easily from the elegant language of mathematics to the same lingua vulgaris with which one might request directions to the restroom. Suffice it to say, while my colleagues in this field obsessively attempt to integrate demonstrably fallible theories in experimental physics on paper, I have been exploring other models in application. They have wasted their lives on concepts in which experiments cannot even be conducted, thereby rendering the term 'experimental physics' a misnomer at best and an oxymoron at the very least, and they will leave this world with nothing more than a thin excreta of publications to their name while I am on the verge of never even having to leave this world. So perhaps your question would be best answered not with calculus or current consensus but rather with a motivational poster from the office supply store. Because I am driven by my will to live, and therein lies your answer, Kenny. By my will and willingness alone, that is how I can do that. Does that answer your question?"

"Well, no," I say. "I didn't mean how can you accomplish it. I meant how can you live with yourself."

He smiles sadly. "Ah, the ubiquitous moral position. Simplistic in its premise, as so many so-called moral conundrums are wont to be, but this one is unusual in that the answer is an inverse perspective on the original question. How can I live with myself? When dying is the only other option, how can I not?"

I hop up on the execution table, the same one where I saw Grazi right after his mind had been wiped, and casually ask: "So why me? You've had plenty of people to test this on, why'd you go to all the effort to bring me back?"

He looks at me like a parent who is taking his child to the sacrificial alter. "Why indeed, and would that I could answer this more eloquently. But while the equations which define physics are founded on the syntax of the calculus, the math with which we measure and describe diversity is unfortunately the same system with which we gamble. I can render anyone a Reset, gifting them with the ability to rewind and edit their lives one fateful day at a time, but I myself wish to move through greater distances in causality, and for that, I will need someone to reset with me while acting as a carrier wave of sorts. And the person who will serve as my vehicle on this journey must have a mind as structurally similar to my own as humanly possible."

He snaps his fingers and points at me, and in response, Peter pushes me down onto the table and starts strapping me in while Prior boosts himself up onto the table next to me. "But while this realization has been a terrible inconvenience for me, you are quite the fortunate one," he continues. "Because unlike my many other subjects, you will not reach your final day only to repeat it indefinitely as I intend to return to a point in your past before our first meeting so that I might use you again and again. Indeed, my dear Kenny, you may very well live forever, as our fates are now inextricably intertwined."

"I guess that makes me lucky, huh?" I say while Peter finishes strapping me in. He gives me a very subtle nod that Prior can't see as he starts to attach electrodes to my scalp. I test the straps and am relieved to know they're not too tight.

"Doubly so I might imagine, as you will not only live forever but you will do so without knowing the cost or means of your immortality. Quite convenient for someone of your pacifistic disposition, wouldn't you agree?"

I'm about to argue that ignorance and coercion aren't part of that ideal, but I'm not here to change his mind any more than he is. So instead I ask "How much of my mind am I going to keep?"

"Ah, that will depend entirely upon you. This isn't your grandfather's paradox, as I am not traveling through time but rather through a sequence of events. And I must say I have become rather vexed with you. When I return to a point in our past, I find myself wondering whether I might rather meet you as you are now, or should I reset you as I erase your mind so that I might replace that vexing version of you with something more docile?"

"You mean if you reset me while you wipe me I'll go back with you? But without any memory of this, like Grazi?"

"Oh, our friend Grazi was one of my first subjects in this phase of the experiment, and it was not a very successful one at that. No, we did not reset Grazi, we merely dropped him off downtown, but otherwise, yes. If I reset you with me, you will return with me, minus most of your memories."

"So either I learn my lesson and don't return with it, or I don't learn my lesson and return without it."

"Such an excellent summarization! This is why I am so fond of you, Kenny. And precisely why I am as conflicted about this as you are. Because while I will not miss your hooliganism, I will most certainly miss these conversations." He smiles at me in the same way I imagine a cat would smile at a mouse while prolonging its life.

It's one thing to kill out of necessity. It's another thing to enjoy it. People skills aren't going to work here. I'm going to have to come back and talk Peter into another plan. "You know what, I just remembered, I think I left the stove on," I say as I pull my arms out of the restraints and the electrodes off my scalp.

"Kenny, you will not survive like this."

"You're right, I won't," I say as I sit up and pull my legs free. "But I'll live." I hop down from the table and walk over to Prior's desk.

"Peter! I require your assistance! Now!" Prior shouts.

I open the top drawer to Prior's desk, take out the gun, and check the chamber. The dull brass cartridge resting in the pipe confirms what Prior already said: this isn't just my first experience with this reality but his as well.

I turn around and level the gun at Prior just as Peter finishes unstrapping him. "Kenny," he says with a stern voice. "When I wake up a few hours ago, I am going to turn the air conditioning to the lowest possible setting and then I am going to turn off all the lights. The last thing you will know before you know nothing will be a desire for warmth..."

I put a bullet through his mouth to shut him up.

"You have any idea how mad he's going to be when he resets?" Peter asks.

"Yeah, well, time for plan B."

"Which is?"

"This was the table Grazi was on, right?"

"Yes."

"Was Santo on this same table?"

He shakes his head. "Doesn't matter, the hardware is the same on both sides. It's the command code that determines who's who."

"What do you mean, who's who?"

"One of you resets, the other one is the carrier wave. Carrier wave gets the juice."

"Can you flip it around and send me back instead of him?"

He nods. "Do you have any idea what's going to happen to me if we fail?" he asks.

"Yes."

"Then why are we even trying?"

"Because we know what will happen if we don't."

I wait and let him mull that over for a moment. I can see the decision in his eyes before he opens his mouth. "I'm not going to remember this. You're going to have to start all over again with me."

"I'm looking forward."

I want to hug him.

Instead, I put the gun to my temple and pull the trigger.

# 74

BAM! The dumpster lid goes down like a gunshot and my eyes pop open. I'm back where I last awoke, in that same old alley behind the Michelin-rated restaurant with the signature saffron marsala sauce and the pasta plates that no one ever seems to finish.

"Shit," Meatball says.

"My friends call me Kenny."

He savors the name like a mouthful of delicious dumpster pasta, then smiles. "Kenny it is. You want something to eat?"

I get up. "No thanks. I have to get to work."

"Oh yeah, another day, another dollar."

"You know what they say, when you live to see another day."

"Are you living?" he asks.

"I am now."

He looks me up and down, then smiles in agreement. "Not a lot of people can say that with that kind of conviction."

"Well, thank you."

"Thank yourself. You sure you don't want to eat something?"

"Next time. Right now, I gotta go work on my people skills."

I excuse myself to go buy a pocket full of meth. The guy Meatball introduced me to a lifetime or reality ago was willing to sell to me even without the introduction, which is good because I don't want Meatball to remember me as a guy who asked for help buying drugs. If I can make it in and out of the hallway to hell just one more time, I'm going to come back here and ask him some more questions.

But on that thought, just in case I don't make it out, I go and get myself a blueberry muffin. And I savor every bite.

Then I hike back to Prior's lab, full of that awful and alive feeling you get when you're not only aware of the ambush but you're running right into it. Unarmed. Some people equate pacifism with cowardice, but I've been under fire enough to know the kind of willpower it takes to keep moving even when you do have a weapon. It takes a lot more when you don't.

I march right through the front door and wait for Peter to appear. He emerges from the stairwell as if on cue and stands there staring at me, as before. I hesitate, in part because he feels like a friend to me now and I know that feeling isn't yet mutual. But also in part because I recognize his fear, and it feels like I'm looking at an old picture of myself.

After a few moments of the world's weirdest staring match, I manage to croak out a question. "Can I ask you something?"

"You want to ask me something?"

I cross the lobby so we can speak in lower tones without the workers overhearing. "Two questions, actually. You got your degree in comparative literature but then you couldn't get a job because no one can connect what you look like with who you are, so you applied to participate in a depression study but got turned down, but then they offered you a job, which you took but which turned into a nightmare where you have to hurt people and the only thing that's saving you from having to choose who gets hurt," I say with a glance over my shoulder at the workers, "is your ability to act like the big dumb loser that everyone thinks they're seeing anyway." I look back at Peter's wide eyes and continue. "So my first question is, if someone in the same predicament were to come along and show you a way out, would you take it?"

He stares at me for an impossibly long minute, his lip quivering as he teeters on the precipice between hope and despair. Then slowly, quietly, he nods.

"Great. Second question," I continue, "do you have any of the keys to any of the other rooms?"

# 75

Now begins the hard part. When I reset Prior, he went back to the last time he woke up, as did I. But while he awoke after three o'clock that same morning, the last time I got up was three days earlier, thanks to the miracle of modern pharmacology. And he doesn't know this, or at least I hope he doesn't. So as of right now, a decision has already been made to let me out after a few days. But when Prior wakes up a couple days from now, that decision will change.

And if that weren't enough to occupy my mind, I'm sitting on the floor of my original room next to the empty frame of a stranger I fell in love with. It's necessary; for this next step to work I need to be able to let myself out, and the downside to Peter's big dumb thug persona is he's only trusted with the bare minimum required to do his job. So he only has his one master key, and he can't be without that for three days while I sit in here alone with Cady's cadaver, which they can't move until the outside of the building is fixed and the workers are all dismissed or buried.

Even with her guts on the outside, I can't help but think she's beautiful. I can't help but feel guilty for dragging her into this, and for failing again and again to pull her back out. And I can't help but wonder where she'd be if she hadn't met me. That guy from the coffee shop doesn't seem so bad after all; at least he could only kill her once.

The weird thing about this meditation trick Meatball taught me is realizing how much effort it takes to drag my mind out of even the ugliest thoughts. But I drag my eyes away from the shell of a woman that was Cady, find a spot on the wall to stare at, and begin my descent into mindfulness by letting that go and focusing on my breathing.

A little less than half a pocket of crystals later, I realize I'm starting to shiver. And it's dark. The air conditioner has been turned on and the lights are off, just as Prior promised. That's my cue.

I produce the key from my pocket, feel my way to the door, and let myself out into the dark and empty hallway. There's a creepy, weird feeling here, like I can hear a chorus of electrical currents in the wires behind the walls humming to me to get the hell out while I can. I look to one side and see the exit sign above the door that leads to the lobby. This is my last chance. My path is clear. I don't have to do this.

I dismiss that thought before it snowballs into an avalanche of anxiety, focus on my breathing for a moment, and when I'm centered and ready, I turn and walk the other way.

Prior looks up as soon as I walk into his lab and his expression goes from arrogance to anger in about the amount of time it takes to blink. I hold my hands up in a defensive posture while offering him the key to my private corner of hell.

"I forgot to return this," I say while placing it gently on the desk by the door.

"Enough of this nonsense!" Prior shouts. He shakes and trembles in pain and rage as he points at me with his cane. "Peter, prepare Mr. Mulligan."

Peter escorts me to the table where Grazi and Santo had their minds wiped while Prior spits and sputters something about how nice it is to see the staff getting along with the lab rats. I'm not even listening to his words as much as to the emotion behind them. There's a lot of pride and anger there, but even more fear and loneliness, and I realize right now that he's spent so much of his life in that state that he doesn't even know he's unhappy. And I suddenly can't help but feel sorry for him. It's one thing to realize that everything he's done to me is an extension of his own pain, it's another thing to realize that I can't save him from it.

Peter starts strapping me in, tugging on each one when he's done. Once he finishes, Prior approaches and starts sticking electrodes on my scalp. "Kenny, I have offered you refuge more than once, and you have turned me down more than I should have allowed, but this. This is unacceptable. You are even less grateful and an even greater nuisance than our erstwhile friend Santo, and that is saying quite a lot."

I smile at his definition of 'refuge,' then I realize he's smiling too, as he tugs down on the straps and tightens me in. I yank and tug on them for real now, unable to pull my arms out, and for just a moment, fear starts to take over. But then I focus on my breathing again and what fills the void in the wake of fear is a deep sadness at what Prior is about to do to himself.

He goes to his desk and takes his gun out, then lifts himself up onto the adjoining table, resting the pistol on his stomach while wiring himself in. I can tell from the way he's looking at me that he's about to lose it, and every time he glances my way it gets worse. We're moving at about the same speed in opposite emotional directions now; he's feeling more anger, I'm feeling more compassion. What we're both feeling is an extension of pain, but the pain is all his.

Once he's finished with his electrodes, he waves his gun around the room while shouting. "Peter! I am ready!"

"You're going to reset me too, aren't you?" I ask.

"For your edification, Kenny, I rather have to now, else on top of reliving just these last few months I might also have to hire more guards to prevent the many inconveniences that you caused. As much as I enjoyed our verbal jousting, I would just as soon save myself the trouble of dealing with a sentient you the next time."

As Peter starts entering commands at the console, I look into Prior's eyes and I start crying. I finally understand what Ellie said all those nights and lifetimes ago; he could stick my head in a blender and the only thing I'd want in this world would be to fix the part of him that sticks peoples' heads in blenders. But I can't fix him. "I am so sorry," I say.

"Well, it is too late for apologies," he spits. Then he turns to Peter and shouts "I said I am ready!"

"It doesn't have to end like this." I know I can't save him, but that doesn't mean I have to stop trying.

"Oh, it is not over. I will see you again soon enough. Part of you, anyway." He turns back to Peter. "Now!"

Peter looks at Prior, then at me. Then he turns around and starts typing furiously. It only takes him a second, but it takes Prior less time than that to realize what he's doing and put a bullet through Peter's back. The shot passes through and out the other side, smashing through the monitor while splattering it with blood.

I start straining in my straps, unable to get out and help as Peter falls forward, almost right into the bloody monitor. He reaches for the return key but Prior puts another bullet into him, followed by another, and another.

Peter staggers and slumps, slips in his own blood and starts to fall, but he catches himself and manages to hang onto the ledge that is the edge of the desk. Prior is screaming something through all the din and the ringing in my ears. But in all his anger, it doesn't occur to him to remove the electrodes from his scalp.

Peter, on his knees now, reaches up to the keyboard. He turns and looks at me, and our eyes connect. I can't move. I can't help. I wouldn't be able to save his life at this point anyway, but it kills me that I can't even comfort him. I realize in this moment that I never hugged him. I never even shook his hand.

He hits the return key and a massive electrical current surges through the electrodes and into Prior's brain. He struggles against the current while trying to reach the electrodes on his scalp but he can't control himself through the convulsions as the electricity overrides his nervous system.

The thing about being electrocuted is, the muscles don't just convulse, they clench inward. And every muscle in Prior's body is doing just that, as his arms and hands curl inward. In one of those hands is a pistol, and on the trigger of that pistol is an index finger. It all happens so fast I almost miss it, but as the electricity overpowers both his body and his will to live, his arm turns the barrel toward his guts while his finger clamps down on the trigger.

I look over and see Peter on the floor now, a gun in his hand, his eyes crossing as he tries with his last ounce of effort to aim for my head. He exhales his last breath and pulls the trigger.

# 76

Bam! My alarm goes off like a gunshot and my eyes slam open. My arm reaches through a blanket that smells like me to find the offending object. Only when it's in my hand do I recognize what I'm holding. It's my old cell phone.

I sit up with alarm and look around at my little cocoon of a studio apartment. There's an overflowing basket of laundry in the corner next to a desk with an old computer that never gets turned on. A stove and a mini fridge sit embarrassingly close to the bathroom door. Against one of the bare walls rests a box of framed photos and certificates. The home of someone struggling with PTSD while living from paycheck to paycheck. My home before I was homeless.

I check the date on my phone and realize it's the day before I first reported to the Prior Institute to interview for the depression study. Or the day before I'll first report; I haven't gone there yet.

I don't know what to do with myself. Everyone I met in the last few weeks, everyone who's died, they're not dead yet, and they don't know me, either. Maybe I'll meet Peter and help him find a job. Maybe I'll find Santo and help him buy a car. But first things first, I'm going to go get some breakfast.

Wait. No. First, I sit down on the floor, find a spot on the wall, and focus on my breathing.

# 77

I step into the coffee shop and take my place in line. A moment later, I feel a presence behind me. I glance back, and there she is; curvy, nerdy, and so beautiful she takes my breath away. I've seen her here before, and we've chatted, but I was too caught up in everything else going on in my life to really notice that she's noticing me.

If I'd known enough to look past the pretty face, I would have seen that she is strong and kind and brave and troubled. She has the sort of look that startles strangers, an appearance that people want to possess.

When people look at her, they see an object, which was why I looked away; I couldn't afford a woman like that. But maybe that's what she kept looking at me while trying to engage me in small talk. Because I didn't act like I was trying to buy her.

She coughs; before, I might have thought she was just clearing her throat, but now I know she's trying to get my attention. My heart is racing, I don't know what to say. I let that thought go and come back to my breathing. That thought comes back, so I let it go again and come back to my breathing. But that thought keeps coming back and it occurs to me that now is a really stupid time to meditate.

I'm about to turn around when my phone buzzes. I take it out of my pocket just as the barista calls out to the next customer in line. The message on my phone is from some guy named Phil. That's right, Phil was my boss. The message says don't come in today, job's been cancelled. That's right, I got laid off. I'm aware of Cady in my peripheral vision pretending she didn't look over my shoulder and see the text. The barista calls out next again, and I'm the next up in line. I reach into my other pocket, suddenly remembering I don't have enough money for both coffee and a muffin. Not like I'm really here for breakfast. I don't really know what I'm here for right now. Maybe I shouldn't wait to meditate after all.

I nod at Cady while counting out change in my hand and she passes me in line. I can't turn around and act like I know her. I can't apologize for getting her killed. I don't know what to do, I can't remember what happens next. I'm used to going back and repeating a day, but not a day that happened so long ago. I focus on my breathing. And then it all comes back to me.

"Next!" the barista shouts.

I run up to the counter, grab the coffee and muffin out of his hands and mutter a quick thanks, then I turn around and weave through the crowd. I can see Cady smiling to herself as I pass her; she doesn't even notice me until I'm holding the door for her.

"Oh! Thank you!" she says, stopping short.

"No, thank you," I say, nodding with my nose at the muffin balanced precariously on top of my coffee. It's not the wisest way to hold these, a strong wind could come through and knock my breakfast over onto the floor. But I wouldn't care, I'm not exactly here for breakfast.

She steps through with a smile and I follow her out onto the sidewalk. It's a beautiful day; the air is crisp, the shadows are long, and everything smells like heaven. Oh wait, that's the muffin that's still precariously balanced on top of my coffee.

"Are you on your way to work?" I ask while redistributing my breakfast between my two hands.

"Yeah. Another day, another dollar."

"Well, you know what they say, when you live to see another day."

She giggles. "In this town? They ask you what you do for a living. Like it defines you or something."

"I know, right? I could die a thousand deaths without ever living if work mattered that much."

Her eyes brighten at this, then she glances at my pocket. The one with the cell phone in it. "Sorry, I. I don't like to pry, but I couldn't help notice. Seems like you got the day off today."

"Oh yeah, but it's just as well. I was thinking of becoming a day trader anyway. Hey, can I walk you to work?"

"Who says I'm going to work?"

"You just..."

She gives me a look that cuts like a bulldozer. "Hello, Mr. I could die a thousand deaths without ever living if work mattered that much. I have a better idea. How about I just act like I'm dying?" She coughs into her hand and starts wheezing like she just came down with the world's fastest case of pneumonia. It's convincing.

She suddenly gets healthy again and beams at me. "I'm Cady, by the way. Cady DeClaire," she says offering me her hand.

I start to balance the muffin on top of the coffee cup again, but it's really precarious, and I'm really afraid I'm going to drop the breakfast she just bought me. I look around for a place to put it, but there isn't a clean surface in sight.

But there's a homeless man sitting on the sidewalk, his head down between his knees. I look at

Cady with pleading eyes; she bought it, so it's her call to make.

She nods. So I set the muffin down on the ground in front of the homeless man, and now, with a free hand, I take hers. "Pleased to meet you, I'm Kenny. Kenny Mulligan."

"Mulligan?" she asks as we fall into step and start walking together. "Does that mean you get unlimited do-overs?"

"Yeah, either that or I suck at whacking balls."

She giggles, then glances back at the homeless man. "Am I going to have to buy you another breakfast?"

"Nah," I say as I pat my pocket and look over my shoulder at the coffee shop. I'm about to say I've got enough for that at least, but right then the homeless man stands up and our eyes connect. It's only for a brief moment before he looks up into the space above and behind me, but in that moment, I recognize him.

It's Ethan Prior.

He smiles, a wet spot blossoming on the front of his pants as he pisses himself.

www.ingramcontent.com/pod-product-compliance
Lightning Source LLC
LaVergne TN
LVHW041058080826
845145LV00007B/1621

*9781737087106*